ENTICED BY HER ISLAND BILLIONAIRE

BECKY WICKS

MILLS & BOON

First published in Great Britain 2020
by Mills & Boon, an imprint of HarperCollins*Publishers*
1 London Bridge Street, London, SE1 9GF
www.harpercollins.co.uk

HarperCollins *Publishers*
1st Floor, Watermarque Building, Ringsend Road
Dublin 4, Ireland

Large Print edition 2021

© 2020 Becky Wicks

ISBN: 978-0-263-28761-5

MIX
Paper from
responsible sources
FSC™ C007454

This book is produced from independently certified
FSC™ paper to ensure responsible forest management. For
more information visit www.harpercollins.co.uk/green.

Printed and bound in Great Britain
by CPI Group (UK) Ltd, Croydon, CR0 4YY

Born in the UK, **Becky Wicks** has suffered with interminable wanderlust from an early age. She's lived and worked all over the world, from London to Dubai, Sydney, Bali, NYC and Amsterdam. She's written for the likes of *GQ*, *Hello!*, *Fabulous* and *Time Out*, a host of YA romance, plus three travel memoirs—*Burqalicious*, *Balilicious* and *Latinalicious* (HarperCollins, Australia). Now she blends travel with romance for Mills & Boon and loves every minute! Tweet her @bex_wicks and subscribe at beckywicks.com.

Also by Becky Wicks

Tempted by Her Hot-Shot Doc
From Doctor to Daddy

Discover more at millsandboon.co.uk.

To my rock star boyfriend Konrad, who is by now quite used to long periods of keyboard tap-tap-tapping before I stop and ask him worrying questions like, 'How much do you think a facelift would cost on a remote island near Bali?' #grateful

CHAPTER ONE

MILA RICCI SWIPED at her thrashing hair as the waves jumped and frothed around the speeding boat. The exclusive transfer by Dr Becker's private yacht from Bali to the island of Gili Indah wouldn't have been quite as bumpy as this, she mused, as a tourist shrieked behind her, but she'd missed it. She'd been advised by an elderly lady with a twinkle in her eyes to sit on the roof of the tourist boat for the next best thing.

The tree-dotted hills in the far distance were pale swathes of varying greens, shrouded by a thin veil of fog in the morning light. The island looked like a painting—just as Annabel had once described it.

Gathering up her red dress, Mila copied the backpackers next to her and dangled her legs over the edge of the roof, resting her arms on the railings. It didn't seem entirely safe by the standards she was used to at home in Britain, but she wasn't worried.

Travelling in potential peril had been standard practice during her time in the Army—especially out in Afghanistan. A few bumpy waves were nothing compared to the time she'd had to take a convoy in the middle of the night and go past the place where the insurgents had burned the bodies of the soldiers they'd shot dead on the bridge.

The direct route to the nearest air station had been just eight miles straight, but they'd gone over a hundred miles around it to escape. Two of the trucks had broken down in the first hour. She'd hitched a ride on another truck and they'd hidden in the sand dunes, listening to the mortar rounds being fired at the vehicle they'd just fled.

Mila rubbed her face. She was tired. She was thinking too much about the past. She couldn't be further from a war zone now if she tried. This was a new start. There was nothing to fear on a paradise island...except maybe a tsunami.

She rolled her eyes at herself at the thought. Why did she always fear the worst?

You know why, she reminded herself. *Because you can't always prepare for the worst, even when you think you can.*

On the deck, an Indonesian man was playing

with a rescued baby monkey. Mark would've got a kick out of that, she thought now, acknowledging the stab of guilt that told her she hadn't ended things with him too well.

She'd been so busy wrapping things up before she'd left the London hospital where she'd devoted herself to her work since leaving the Army. She'd barely had a moment even to think about him since she'd broken things off. He was a good man, but maybe a little too soft for her. He didn't know how to handle her.

What was it Mark had said before he'd left her flat? *'You don't need a man right now anyway, Mila. You need to figure out who you are.''*

He was probably right about that. She hadn't come home from Afghanistan the same person. She'd learned quickly out there who she really was. She was part of a team and she couldn't fail. She was eyes, ears, instincts. She was ready for the worst—always.

She could still hear the whirring rotors of the helicopters infiltrating the hot, sticky night air. When she least wanted to she could conjure up the smell of dust and the acrid stench of wet blood on inconceivably terrible wounds. The agonised moans of broken soldiers still made it into her dreams some nights.

It had been more than her twenty-four-year-old self had known how to handle at the time she'd been deployed, though she'd never admitted that to anyone. It had only been after her twin Annabel's death, eight years later, that she'd truly fallen apart.

Mila watched two Australian lads making faces at the monkey, but she wasn't really paying attention. She was dreading the anniversary of her sister's death all over again. It was almost three years ago now since the accident.

She'd been home on leave for a few weeks when it had happened. Annabel had been trying to lift her spirits, keeping her one step ahead of depression after her latest posting to Afghanistan. But for all of Mila's Army training, and everything she'd endured in combat, she'd still frozen on the spot when she'd come across her mother's twisted, unrecognisable car, smashed just like the motorbike Annabel had hit before wrapping the car around a tree.

Those wasted seconds she'd spent, willing the steel of the car to unwind, willing the clock to go back, might have been the difference between her sister's life or death. The worst thing had happened and she hadn't been prepared. She'd failed to get Annabel out alive.

'There they are!'

Mila blinked as a voice shrieked excitedly behind her. A backpacker in a red football shirt was pointing at the islands, coming ever closer to them. They were headed for the largest of those several small bumps in the ocean, which jutted like camel humps ahead of them.

Adrenaline spiked in her veins. She willed herself not to think about Afghanistan, or the accident. But she knew Annabel would be here too; she was everywhere.

Annabel had actually come to Gili Indah without her years ago. She and her twin had planned the trip together, but Mila had come down with an unfortunate case of laryngitis just before the flight. She could still remember that crackly phone call from her twin.

'You've got to see it one day, Mila! The most beautiful mountain views...the blue of the water... it's unreal! And there are loads of hot men here. You're missing out, I can tell you.'

Was it a coincidence that this opportunity to spend the next couple of months or so at the prestigious Medical Arts Centre there—or the MAC, as it was known—had appeared in her online searches, just last month?

The MAC hadn't been there at the time of Annabel's visit, six and a half years ago. It would have been a mere gleam in the eye of its founder, the billionaire Dr Sebastian Becker. He'd left his whole celebrity surgeon lifestyle behind in Chicago only three years ago, to set up this exclusive facility.

Mila watched the monkey peel its own banana, its tail wrapped around one of the Australian guys' forearms.

What was he like? she mused. This man Dr Becker?

Her friend Anna back at the hospital in London had told her a little about him, but only what she'd garnered from watching him on TV.

The Becker Institute—Dr Becker's revered plastic surgery practice in Chicago—was the base for a globally popular reality TV show focused on the lives of its patients and their various cosmetic surgery procedures.

Dr Becker had only starred in one season, with his brother Jared Becker, before leaving the show to concentrate on building the MAC. Anna had said he'd really left because the media circus had got too much for him. Something about an ex-girlfriend, threats, scandal...

Mila had stopped her there. She hated listening to gossip. And it had felt wrong to poison her mind about a man she'd never met—especially a man who was doing such remarkable work.

Dr Sebastian Becker had pioneered what was now the world's leading method of scar tissue surgery, blending the newest innovative laser treatment with a simplified but highly effective surgical procedure. This was the first time he'd offered an opportunity for another experienced surgeon to come to the clinic for a short-term placement and observe his techniques.

It had sounded fascinating to her—the chance to learn something new at his exclusive private island clinic—and she hadn't hesitated to hand in her notice at the London hospital.

Indonesia was surely bound to be a far nicer setting than an overwhelmed city hospital or a military hospital in the Middle East. She was done with all that. She'd come for something completely different—a new focus, a change of pace, even if it was only temporary.

She couldn't even recall what Dr Sebastian

Becker looked like, or the name of the TV show he'd so briefly starred in. She'd never had much time for TV, and she didn't ever bother with social media. Hopefully the man was agreeable, at least; they'd be working in pretty close proximity.

Mila smoothed her red sundress and held her hair back as the wind wrestled with it. She wished she could have asked Annabel what to expect from this place beyond the gorgeous guy she'd met when she had been here. What had she said his name was? Bas...or something like that?

Sebastian Becker hauled the last remaining tank out of the water and eyed the speedboat heading his way. He reached down to help the first of his dive group back onto the boat. Getting them all on board before the next intake of tourists whipped up the water was imperative if he didn't want his students flailing in opposite directions within seconds.

'Give me your hand.'

Gabby, a British woman in her early twenties, pushed her mask down to her neck and grinned up at him from the water. 'I'll give you whatever you need.'

He helped her up the ladder and she fell against his chest, heavy and wet in her tank and vest.

'Sorry,' she muttered, so close to his face he could feel her breath on his skin.

She wasn't sorry. This girl had been flirting with him all morning.

He helped the others up. Checking his students were seated and had disposed of their flippers in the right place, he yelled, 'Ketut, start the engine!' and bounded up the three metal rungs to the roof.

Alone, he unzipped his wetsuit, letting the thick wet fabric unfold around his middle. The sun sizzled on his skin.

Maybe tonight, when the last scheduled surgery was done, he'd take Gabby out for a drink, somewhere with candles and a sandy floor. She'd be gone in a day or two. Why not give her something to talk about, once her plane deposited her back into her boring existence?

Those had been her words this morning, not his.

'My life is so boring compared to yours. I should stay here and just go scuba diving all day with you...what do you think?'

He hadn't encouraged her. Why tell a stranger

that he wasn't only a scuba diver, either? Why tell a tourist he would never see again that he was actually living here because he'd pioneered a way of operating on the facial scarring of accident victims which minimised their scars often to near invisibility?

He thought back to last week, satisfied. Lasers were incredible things. Trevor Nolan, a forty-two-year-old wedding singer from Dakota, had grappled with his young son to prevent a firework going off in his face and the poor guy had taken the hit himself. After six months of surgery and a month of crowdfunding by his friends he come to him at the MAC for what all the medical journals were calling 'revolutionary treatment.'

Trevor had left with his chin almost the shade of the rest of his face, instead of raw red and stretched in scars. Best of all, he could sing for people again without it hurting.

'Mr Diver Man, come down here!'

Gabby was calling him from below. He stayed put. The sun at this time of the day was perfect. Not too hot. He liked to soak it up while he could, before he put his hospital scrubs back on.

Sebastian assumed most people visiting the island's clubs and bars and dive shops didn't even know the MAC was on the other side of it, and if they did most of them didn't know what happened there.

He always let word of mouth bring his clients in now. He wasn't famous on Gili Indah. He wasn't followed and he was barely recognised. It was too small an island and he was too out of context, he supposed—a world away from the Institute in Chicago and all those cameras.

He still had to be careful on the mainland of nearby Bali, though.

He'd left the hugely successful *Faces of Chicago* show back home. He'd left Klara behind, too, he told himself, furrowing his brow at the horizon. Now all that mattered was his team, and having his patients walking away looking and feeling better than when they'd arrived.

The speedboat was close now. A few faces stood out—locals, friends. And lots of new arrivals. But none for the MAC. *His* staff came in on *his* boat.

All but Dr Ricci, he remembered suddenly, raking a hand through his hair. She'd missed her transfer, which wasn't uncommon—the traffic on the mainland was a nightmare.

He stood, scanning the other boats around the bay. He'd been too swamped at work to search online and put a face to the name of his latest employee, but he knew she'd worked in trauma on deployment with the Army in Afghanistan, so she was likely looking to add a new scar treatment string to her bow.

He considered what it must be like to spend months in a war zone, seeing soldiers with their limbs blown to shreds. All those gunshot wounds, severed bones and bombs exploding…

Some of the things he'd had to fix himself had been far worse than Trevor Nolan's chin after his battle with a rocket in his backyard. But to be in a war zone—that was something else.

The boat jolted and he heard a tank flip downstairs. He shot back down the ladder. This woman, Dr Ricci, must be some kind of special breed. What was she looking for, exactly, here on such a remote island?

He set the tank upright again and watched Gabby make a show of resting her bare pink toes on it to keep it in place. Ketut threw him a look from behind the wheel, and Sebastian took a seat as far away from her as he could.

Was Dr Ricci running from the horrors of war

and looking for peace, like he had been? But he'd been running from the media explosion after starring in the TV show and from the guilt that had racked him over what had happened to Klara. Hardly the same thing.

Sebastian realised he was scowling at the horizon, thinking about Klara again.

He couldn't have known what would happen after filming started. No one could have anticipated so many photographs, so many camera lenses zooming in on his every move, in and out of surgery. All those headlines and sub-headlines…the crazy stories people had sold or made up about them just to get their clicks in.

Letting cameras into his surgery had invited the whole damn media circus in—which had squeezed every last remaining shred of joy out of his relationship with Klara.

All she had ever wanted to do was be with the kids at her kindergarten school and live a simple happy life with him. She had been so broken by the invasion of her privacy, and everything people had said about them both as a couple, that at the end she'd left without saying goodbye.

He put a hand down to the ocean spray and let his thoughts about her go—like he did every time he went diving. Diving was a workout for his brain...a place to switch off from other thoughts. It was only when he was on the surface that the memories came back.

He knew Klara wasn't in Chicago any more. She'd already got married—someone she'd met in Nepal. He didn't know where she was now, but he was happy for her. Sometimes.

Right now he would much rather be living here, somewhere beautiful, fixing Trevor Nolans and kids with burns the size of basketballs on their cheeks, than go back to having camera flashes and the paparazzi's car tyres screeching in his wake, and performing endless boob jobs in Chicago. Although he wished he could see his family more often—especially his brother Jared and Charlie... He smiled thinking of his nephew.

The tourist boat slowed. A line of excited people craned their necks from the roof to the turquoise shallows. Everyone was in awe of the colour of the water here.

A slender woman in a bright red sundress had her hand on her brown hair, trying her best to tame it, and a memory flickered across his mind.

He lifted his sunglasses and squinted to see better.

She was leaning on the railings now, elbows out. Her sundress was catching her ankles in the wind. He gripped the side of the boat even as Gabby tickled his calf with her toes. It looked *exactly* like her. Must be six or seven years ago now… A British woman dancing drunken pirouettes on the sand, back when he'd been here for the first time—long before he'd even had the idea to build the MAC.

What was *she* doing back here?

Mila's eyes followed the diver right until his boat rocked out of sight. His abs were like a digitally enhanced ad for a diving school. She'd seen men like that at military hospitals, trained for fighting but battered and blue. Never this colour. The diver's skin was a warm shade of caramel—as if he'd earned that tan with a life outdoors over a long, long time.

Her boat bobbed in the shallows as people leapt from the sides onto the sand. Mila followed, taking the ladder down. She hoisted her sundress further up her legs as an eager Indonesian boy no older than eight or nine helped her down into an inch of crystal-clear water.

'Terima kasih!' she told him. She'd already mastered a few basics.

The warmth of the sand rose to meet her toes in her flip-flops and she breathed in the scent of the air. Flowers…maybe jasmine…or was that an incense stick? The local market on a dusty path ahead told her she wasn't exactly in Robinson Crusoe territory.

Mila stood still. When was the last time she'd stood in the ocean? Probably back in Cornwall, about twenty years ago. She'd been with her mum and Annabel, and they'd bought Cornish pasties and prodded jellyfish in the sand. That had been a good day.

'Can I help you, miss? You need room?'

The kid in front of her now looked about seventeen, and he seemed to want to deny her the pleasurable personal moment of feeling her feet in the ocean for the first time in twenty years. He waded over purposefully and helped drag her case away from the shore.

She studied his tattooed wrists as he flashed a ring binder at her, showing coloured photographs of accommodation options. 'Oh, no, thank you. I have a hotel for tonight.'

'I have better one!' He flicked to a page with

a photo of a shack on it. It looked basic, to say the least.

'Tomorrow I move to the MAC,' she explained, wading onto the beach. Tiny bits of coral prodded at her heels and toes.

Mila took her case back quickly. She had probably divulged too much information already. It was never good to trust strangers on a first encounter unless in a medical situation. Besides, she already knew Dr Sebastian Becker kept a low profile.

He encouraged his staff to do the same.

For protection, when it comes to our clients' anonymity.

He'd written that in a welcome email.

'Taxi?' she said in vain as a horse and cart trotted past her on the dusty street.

'Watch out!'

The teenager was back. He caught her elbow and yanked her to the side of the path just as another horse and cart rattled past at full speed. It almost struck her.

'Thank you, I'm fine.'

She picked up her fallen sunglasses. She wanted to tell him she could take care of herself but she refrained. He was only being chivalrous and she *had* been caught off-guard. She hadn't slept in almost two days.

Frazzled and sweating, she wheeled all her worldly belongings along the thick, dusty, pot-holed concrete that constituted a street.

Street food vendors were mixing noodles and jabbing straws into coconuts. Girls were swigging beer, pedalling bicycles in bikinis. The salty air was already clinging to her forehead. No one else offered to help her but that was OK. She'd done this before, in worse places. She just hadn't imagined the island would be this crowded...

Through the jet lag she remembered that she'd come in on a tourist boat, to the tourist side of Gili Indah. The MAC was on the west side. That part of the island was exclusive territory—just for patients and staff. She couldn't wait to dive into a swimming pool. She just had to wait until tomorrow...

Mila was about to hail the approaching horse and cart when a noise from the shore made her stop in her tracks. A shriek. Someone thrashing in the waves.

Squinting through the throng, her eyes fell on a girl a few metres behind the speedboat. She saw the yellow dive boat she'd seen before, from the water. Something must have happened.

'Snake!' Gabby screamed. 'It bit me! Ow, it hurts! Sebastian, help!'

'OK…it's OK. Let's get you back to shore.'

Sebastian looped an arm around her waist, turning his head in all directions, looking at the shallows. Where was the snake?

One minute Gabby had been heading back from the boat right next to him, after their second dive, the next she'd been toppling over in her half-undone wetsuit.

He made a grab for her mask and fins before they were swept out of reach, and threw them to another guy in their group.

'There it is!' Gabby sounded horrified.

He followed her pointing finger to the thin, yellow and black stripy body of a sea snake. It wriggled past him, heading for the deep beyond the reef.

Sebastian tried to wade faster. Gabby's face had turned pale. She wasn't making this up.

'Where did it bite you?' He kept his voice controlled, not wanting to panic her. Her head was heavier every time it landed on his shoulder.

'On my foot…my foot!' She was sobbing now, barely able to breathe.

'Ketut!' he yelled.

Gabby's legs seemed to crumple underneath her on the sand. He caught her before she could fall and lowered her gently to her back on the sand. She was whimpering now, trying to clutch at his arm. Her face was almost white.

A frenzy of people crowded around. Some were even snapping the scene with their cameras.

'Get back,' he ordered gruffly, as the familiar surge of contempt for this kind of privacy invasion consumed him. 'Ketut!' he called again.

But someone else was already sprinting over.

'I'm a doctor—how can I help?'

The lady in red from the boat. The British tourist. It was definitely her…the woman from a few years ago. Speechless, he watched as she dropped to her knees.

'Snake bite,' she noted out loud, before he could explain. She put a hand to Gabby's ankle.

'Yeow!' Gabby clamped her hand around his wrist in a death grip.

Easing her fingers away, he helped his new partner adjust the bitten leg and support it on an upturned rock.

'We need pressure immobilisation,' she told him—as if he didn't know.

She started pulling things from her bag. Her sunglasses were pushed high on her head, sweeping back the kind of thick honey-brown hair he'd bet smelled good wet, right after she showered...

He caught himself, racking his brain for her name.

They hadn't done more than flirt a little back then. If his memory served him right there had been no chemistry between them whatsoever. She'd been a drinker, he hadn't, and she'd been intent on partying every night until she dropped.

But he never forgot a face. Had she really forgotten his?

'Do you know what to do?' she asked him.

Her wide-set eyes were a vivid blue in the sun, over high, freckled cheekbones.

'There's anti venom at the clinic,' he said.

'At the Medical Arts Centre?'

He lost his voice for a second. Up close, he smelled the coconut waft of her sunscreen.

'No, the other one—the Blue Ray Medical Clinic on the strip.'

Didn't she recognise him at all? Was it even her? But, yes, it had to be. Her eyes, her face...

they were all so familiar. He just couldn't remember her name.

'What will you do to me?' Gabby cried out.

'You need to keep as still as you can,' he said. 'Stop the venom circulating.'

The Brit…what *was* her name?…raised an eyebrow. Her blue eyes gave his body a swift appraisal in his wetsuit.

'You're a doctor?'

'You could say that.' He watched her pull an elastic bandage from her bag. 'The clinic's next to the Villa Sunset Hotel. It wasn't here before.'

'Before…?'

Her hands worked quickly, wrapping the elastic bandage around Gabby's leg with deft efficiency, starting from her toes, moving swiftly up to her thigh.

He sprinted to the restaurant right by the harbour. Their fence was made up of pieces of piled-up driftwood—just the right size for a splint.

'Use this,' he said, dropping back down next to her.

'Perfect—thanks.'

She was impressively fast. She *looked* like the girl he'd met before, but she sure as hell wasn't *acting* like her. Her red dress was catching dirt but she didn't look as if she cared or even noticed as they loaded a sobbing Gabby into the back of a cart. His eyes lingered on the curve of her shoulder as one strap fell down to her arm. She caught his eye and yanked the strap up.

'Come with me, *please*,' Gabby begged him.

The Brit answered instead. 'I'll go with you. We need to take the pressure off your leg as much as possible in this cart, though. Can you work with me on that?'

'I'll try.'

'I'll help you.'

She was good with her patient. Sebastian helped her arrange the leg, waiting for any hint that she might remember him.

'The driver knows where to go,' he told her. 'I'll follow on my bike. Tell them I sent you.'

'And your name is…?'

'Sebastian Becker?' He said it like a question as he slid the lock shut at the back of the cart.

Her blue eyes grew wide in shock. 'Dr… Becker?'

Finally. He opened his mouth to say something about the coincidence of another encounter all these years later. But he couldn't exactly admit to her that he'd forgotten her name.

It was only after she'd disappeared in a cloud of dust that he finally remembered it.

Annabel.

CHAPTER TWO

'SHE NEEDS ANTI-VENOM,' Mila called out, hurrying through the doors of the Blue Ray Clinic.

She flashed her security card at a man in the small, busy lobby. The bearded Indonesian man in his mid to late fifties sprang into action. The name badge on his white coat read *Agung*.

In a white room off the hallway, the tiled floor squeaked under her flip-flops. 'Sea snake,' she told Agung. He was already observing the bandage. 'She needs anti-venom. Dr Becker will be here any second. I'm Dr Mila Ricci—I'm new at the MAC. I just met him at the harbour.'

That scuba diving poster model in a wetsuit—that *doctor*—was the surgeon she'd soon be working with.

She was still in shock.

She closed the door behind them, noting the fresh paint on the cream walls and the Indonesian art hanging by the window. A palm leaf tapped at the glass from outside.

They helped the still dripping girl to a bed and onto fading sheets. Her breathing was laboured—probably due to her writhing around, not to the venom spreading too much. But then, she hadn't stayed very still in the jostling cart, even with Mila's assistance.

A rush of air-conditioning blasted her face as the door swung open to admit Dr Becker. 'Agung, how's she doing?'

He was pulling on a white coat, arm by long, bulked-up arm, and striding towards the bed in black sports sandals. He was every bit as striking in the white coat as he was in a wetsuit.

He made to pass her, then stopped, placed a hand on her shoulder. 'Thank you for what you just did.'

'You're welcome.'

The words came out smoothly, calmly, as she'd intended, but she didn't feel calm. The look he was giving her now had suspicion all over it.

'Put this on,' he told her, throwing her a white coat from a hook on the wall. 'Nurse Viv is with another patient, so I hope you won't mind staying a bit longer. I need you to cut the suit,' he said, motioning to the pair of scissors on the tray.

Mila snipped carefully at the girl's wetsuit and

discarded the flimsy material. She was following commands when she'd usually be giving them, but that was OK. She wasn't a hundred miles away from base in Ghazni. No one had been blasted by shrapnel from a rocket-propelled grenade, There were no wounded soldiers crying out for attention. There was only this one girl… right here, right now.

She put a gentle hand to Gabby's leg and soothed her as Dr Becker administered the antivenom and the meds kicked in.

Agung's pager made a sound. 'Excuse me, Dr Becker… Dr Mila,' he said.

He left the room and instantly the air grew thicker. Sebastian was appraising her again.

'Mila?' he said in a surprised voice, as soon as it was only the two of them. He stepped towards her.

'She looks much better,' she told him, looking up to see his eyes narrow. 'I think we got to the bite just in time. She just needs to rest now.'

He folded his arms, towering over her. He must be at least six foot two inches to her five foot three.

'Why Mila? I thought your name was Annabel?'

All the breath left her body.

'I couldn't remember at first...back there. It was at least six or seven years ago, right? Before this clinic or the MAC existed,' he said. 'You were late to our snorkelling party—you'd had too much to drink, remember?'

He grinned, laughing at a memory that wasn't hers.

Tears stung her eyes. She could have wrestled him to the ground when he reached for her wrists, but his long, tanned fingers ran gently over her scars and she felt bolted to the floor.

He was turning her arms in the harsh overhead light, studying the faint silvery lines as if they were clues to a mystery game. 'You didn't have these before,' he said, frowning. 'What happened to you?'

She bit her cheeks as the tears threatened to spill over. *He'd met Annabel.* This must be the guy her sister had come back talking about all those years ago. Bas. Sebastian. It made sense now. Dr Sebastian Becker was Bas. And she had to work with him?

She had to set him straight. This was unbearable.

'I'm not...not who you think I am,' she managed. The room felt suddenly way too small.

She took a step back, pulling her arms away. 'Dr Becker, I'm Dr Mila Ricci. I've come to work at the MAC for a while and learn your techniques. I would have met you earlier, but I missed my transfer. I apologise for the confusion.'

She watched him rake a hand through his hair as she struggled for composure.

He paced the room, then stopped. 'Am I going crazy here? I did meet you before, didn't I? Did you change your name?'

'I'm not Annabel,' she said through a tight throat. 'Annabel was my twin sister. She's dead, Dr Becker. She died three years ago. It was her you met—not me.'

The cat padded her way across the bar towards them, its black shiny fur glowing pink under the LED lights. Sebastian ran a hand along her soft back. 'I'm so sorry about the mix-up this morning,' he said to the woman in front of him, his newest albeit temporary employee.

He'd been thinking about her all day. He'd sent Mila to her hotel to get some sleep and had somehow kept things on schedule back at the MAC, even though his mind had been whirring. He'd even checked in quickly on Gabby, back at the Blue Ray, who was fine. She'd found the strength to ask for his number, but he had no intention of entertaining her now. He just wanted to clear things up with Mila.

'It's not your fault. It's a coincidence and a surprise, that's all. Annabel talked about meeting a guy called Bas—I just didn't put the pieces together.'

Mila's legs were crossed in his direction on the swing seat beside him.

'What's her name?' she asked, watching his fingers stroke the length of the cat's tail.

'This is Kucing. I found her when she was a kitten. Someone dumped her in the garbage can down by the bottle store. Nice, huh? She was in a real sorry state—weren't you, girl?'

Kucing rubbed her nose against his fingers and promptly sat down to lick her tail.

'She likes it here. The guys give her tuna from the can on Wednesdays.'

He watched Mila reached out a hand to rub the cat's ears. The scars across her wrists glinted in the light of the candle in a coconut shell.

'Why is she called Kucing?'

'It's Indonesian for cat.' He shrugged. 'We like to keep things simple around here.'

Reggae drifted in from the speakers outside on the palm trees. Ketut's wife, Wayan, slid two empty glasses across the bar towards him, followed by a jug of ice water. It wasn't a fancy bar, more a rustic boho shack, but it was usually quiet—which was why he liked it. He hoped Mila was OK. It was hard to gauge how his new recruit was really feeling about this mix-up.

'It was brief. Meeting your sister, I mean,' he said.

She nodded, her eyes still on the cat. It was surreal. She looked absolutely identical to Annabel. He still couldn't believe it. He didn't recall Annabel ever telling him she was a twin—not that they'd really spent much time together.

'How did she die? Is it OK if I ask?'

'She went out one night to a party,' Mila said slowly, without looking at him. 'She was driving our mum's car...'

'You mean she died in a car crash? I'm so sorry. Was she alone in the car?'

Mila stiffened, picked up her drink. 'I don't really want to talk about this now, if that's all right with you. I'm here to work, Dr Becker, to focus on what's here and now—not on what happened in the past. What's the deal with the Blue Ray Clinic, by the way? Do you work there too?'

'I drop by if I'm needed. And I've done some work on the place. It was more of a shack when I got here,' he said, admonishing himself for prying. 'Look, we don't have to talk about the accident if you don't want to.'

'Thank you.'

Mila had changed from the red dress into a long, pleated pale blue skirt and a low-cut white top. He assumed her slender frame would look good in most things—including an Army uniform. She had an air of sophistication about her, he mused. And a bluntness, too. It was unequivocally British—like her accent.

He'd only met her twin a few times when she was here, but Annabel had been very different. She had danced in a skin-tight dress and drunk tequila shot after shot, hogging the microphone on karaoke night. He couldn't picture *this* woman doing that, somehow.

He felt a slight awkwardness between them as she petted Kucing. 'You don't have to call me "Dr Becker", by the way, Sebastian is just fine,' he said, to break the silence.

'OK—Sebastian.' She smiled slightly, tucking

her hair behind her ear. 'So, you also teach scuba diving? Sounds like you have a lot on your plate.'

'That's what happens, I guess, on an island. You kind of end up taking on a little bit of everything.'

He ordered them both a smoothie—the house speciality. He didn't think of his efforts at Blue Ray as anything different from his work at the MAC any more. He was just living his life, doing what was necessary to keep things moving.

He still harboured some small hope that one day Jared would leave Chicago and join him here, but that would mean the rest of his family giving up the show and all the fame that came with it.

His brother was a little different from him where that was concerned. Jared and his wife Laura hadn't come under half as much scrutiny as he and Klara had. He assumed that because they'd already been married a while they weren't as exciting. They had never been splashed on magazine covers or stopped for trick photos outside jewellery stores.

'From what I know about your background, I could probably learn some things from *you*, Dr Ricci,' he said now, shoving away the thought of the time he'd been stopped by someone pretending to be homeless just so that someone else could get a photo of him reportedly shopping for an engagement ring. Up to that point he hadn't even considered proposing to Klara, but the pressure from the public had been on after that.

'Call me Mila, please,' she said, scanning his eyes now with her vivid blue ones. 'What do you know about my background, exactly?'

'I know from your résumé that you risked your life in Afghanistan,' he said.

She looked vaguely amused. 'I was safe most of the time.'

'And I know you know your way out of an awkward situation.'

She paused, a half-smile still playing on her lips. 'Well, I'll let you think you know about me for now. So we don't make things even more awkward.'

Were they *flirting*? For a second it felt as if she was flirting with him. With any other woman it would already feel like a date.

'So, why did you sign up for the Army?' He poured ice water into her glass, watched Kucing nuzzle her chin and then snake around the coconut shell candle. 'Did you always want to end up out there in a combat zone?'

'I joined the Army reserve for money, plain and simple.'

She twirled the ice cubes in her glass. He noticed her nails—plain, neat, unpainted. Her earrings—tiny silver studs.

'I thought it would help me to pay for medical school. I was only twenty-four and my plans were rock-solid—you know what it's like when you're young.'

'Did you have any choice when you found out where you were going?' he asked curiously. He hadn't met too many women who'd spent so long in military service.

'I didn't question it. I knew what I'd signed up for. We trained for four months before we left for Afghanistan and I was sent to two forward-operating bases as part of a mobile surgical team. Straight in at the deep end.'

'You only trained for four months?'

She nodded. 'Four long months of saying good-byes and firing hand grenades…'

Sebastian felt his eyes widen.

'You think I couldn't still fire a hand grenade if I really needed to?' she teased.

He found the idea vaguely arousing, somehow. He cleared his throat, took a sip of the smoothie Wayan had presented him with.

'Annabel was out of her mind when I told her they were placing me close to the frontline,' Mila continued. 'We all thought I'd be on the base in Bagram—not some tiny outpost. On the plane it kind of hit me like a bomb—no pun intended… That's the only time I thought I might die out there.'

'How do you even train for something like that?' he asked, watching her lips close around the bamboo straw in her smoothie. She looked at him over the rim of her glass.

'We had to kick down doors, do escape and evasion stuff, urban combat manoeuvres—a lot of things that were probably unnecessary, now that I think about it.'

'Like the hand grenade lessons?'

She shrugged. 'Those actually came in handy. I just wanted to be the toughest soldier and the best trauma surgeon I could be—and it didn't feel like more than I could handle to be both those things. I enjoyed the training. I wanted to be the face of resilience and strength, you know? I wanted to be the one who could keep her cool in the middle of all that…' she paused. 'All that horror…all those soldiers with devastating wounds. So devastating, Sebastian. So pointless.'

'I can't imagine,' he said.

Her lips were pursed, as if she was trying not to let any more emotion than necessary escape with her words.

'Every patient that came to us was critical,' she said. 'I do miss that type of patient care sometimes. The teamwork out there is like nothing else I've ever experienced. The things you go through you're not going to go through anywhere else.'

He found he was listening intently, as if she was taking him on a journey. He almost forgot where he was.

'It's an adrenaline rush, you know? But you're still human at the end of the day. I exercised it out—all the excess trauma that felt like it was spreading from them straight into me. I ran miles on the treadmill every day to get it all out, but I still cried every night in the shower.'

Sebastian was silent. What the hell could he say?

'You never really stop seeing it,' she told him. 'I'm not going to lie to you: it took a lot to get over that stuff. But not as much as it took to get over my sister's death. I was home on leave when the accident happened, and after that I got out as soon as I could.'

Mila ran her hands through her hair, revealing those scars again. He didn't dare ask again how she'd got those; she'd recoiled from him in horror when he'd examined them before.

'Like I said, I'm here now to be *here*—present. I don't see why the past should affect what I'm doing,' she said, sitting up straighter.

He wondered if she really believed that.

'So, tell me something about *your* life, Dr Becker. Why did you move your skills so far away from Chicago and from the States in general?'

He sat back. He hadn't been expecting such directness. 'You don't read the news?'

'News always finds me eventually, if it's important.'

'Interesting perspective on communication,' he said dryly. She was fascinating. 'But, seriously, you never even looked me up on the internet after I hired you? You don't know about the infamous, record-breaking, highly rated—or should I say *overrated*—TV show *Faces of*

Chicago? Or how the "scorned Becker brother" left town after only one season, all alone…?'

She slowly spun her glass on the bar, with one finger on the rim. 'I don't follow celebrity news or social media.'

'I don't have social media accounts any more,' he told her, wondering what it was, exactly, that was making him feel the need to earn her respect before he left this bar stool.

She met his eyes. 'I know about your work. I know you've spent three years revolutionising your facial scarring reduction procedure out here—mostly alone. I know your skills had brought unprecedented fortune to The Becker Institute in Chicago even before the TV show brought you fame. Was it your father's practice?'

'Late father,' he said. 'He passed away.'

'I'm sorry.'

'Thank you.'

She didn't ask how, or when it had happened, but she looked for a moment as if she wanted to.

'If I'm honest,' she said, and sighed, 'a friend filled me in on some things about your personal life which may or may not be true… I always prefer to ask people about this sort of thing to their face, if I need to. I wasn't anywhere near a television when your show was on.'

'I'm sure you had better things to do than watch me and my brother performing tummy tucks on spoilt pop stars anyway.'

'I'm not sure that's true...' she said thoughtfully.

Kucing leapt back on the bar and padded straight towards Mila, almost knocking over her smoothie glass. She caught it deftly, avoiding any spillage.

'It would have been nice to switch off and see what else was happening out there in the world. Some nights the silence was worse than the sound of the guns firing.'

Not for the first time in her company, Sebastian found himself speechless.

'Sorry,' she said, shaking her head in bewilderment. 'Talking about this is a bit of a Pandora's box. I don't want you to think I'm always like this. I'm just tired. Back to you?'

He was stumped. There was a lot he wanted to say, but he didn't know where to start. So he just said, 'I very much look forward to working with you, Mila. I just hope the island and the MAC live up to your expectations.'

'I try not to have any preconceived expectations,' she told him. 'So… I'm guessing you really didn't like being on that show?'

Sebastian tipped the ice cubes in his glass to one side and back again. She had a lot of questions. 'It wasn't so much the show I didn't like—more the way the media ate us up. They're vicious out there…hiding in the shadows, waiting to pounce.' He made his hands like a cat's paws and she smiled.

'I know a bit about people like that,' she said.

He hoped she wouldn't talk about Klara, but even if she knew anything about her she didn't ask.

'So you still take the high-paying clients if they seek you out here? The celebrities?' she asked.

'Yes. They like the luxury of the island. But I do also have plans for a place over in Bali—a wellness centre for trauma patients in recovery. Something a little less…expensive. We have to start reaching more people.'

'You seem to have things under control,' she said. 'Your brother Jared—is he involved here too?'

'He's still busy being a television star,' he said, hoping he didn't sound as if he begrudged his older brother the life he'd chosen in the spotlight. 'We should get a snack—I'm hungry.'

He ordered them chips, then moved the topic to a patient who was heading in for a routine penis enlargement. Anything seemed better than bringing up his family issues. They were small fry compared to what this woman had been through.

So she talked, and he listened, and Sebastian couldn't even remember when he'd met a woman quite like Mila. She was definitely going to keep him on his toes.

CHAPTER THREE

'I'M OPEN TO SUGGESTIONS, Dr Becker. What do you think might improve...this?'

The woman in the plush leather chair opposite them stretched out the skin on her cheeks with her fingers. Mila watched Sebastian push his glasses further up the bridge of his nose.

'Turn to the left, please,' he said. 'Now the right.'

Incense swirled from the polished window ledge of the cosy, bamboo-panelled consultation room. It floated about his thick dark hair as he studied their patient's face. Mila fought not to look too long at his handsome profile in the sunlight.

It was already a week since she'd first stepped through the high-arching, intricately hand-crafted doors of the Medical Arts Centre, and she'd been transfixed by everything in it ever since.

This facility was a world away from the Blue

Ray Clinic, which she'd noticed still looked a little rough around the edges in places. Everything about the polished marble floors, the potted palms and golden vases spoke of peace and control. It was the least traumatic place for a trauma victim she'd ever seen. It was as if she'd fallen asleep in the back seat of a convoy truck, been pelted with an AK-47, and then woken up here.

Rachel, their bubbly radiology technician, who had a penchant for wearing pink sandals around the place, had told her they hadn't remodelled the entire Blue Ray Clinic yet because Sebastian was funding everything himself.

'Rumour has it there are problems in the Becker family, and it all started with the show. Did you know his brother Jared has never even been out to visit the island?'

Mila had remained quiet—she wasn't about to join in gossip. But she had found something else the other woman had said rather intriguing:

'I heard that Dr Becker was so devastated about his ex-girlfriend after she left him that he used to fly out of here every weekend to go and try to find her.'

There was a lot of gossip going around this island about everything, she'd noticed. And she couldn't help wondering what was true about Sebastian and what wasn't. She'd enjoyed their chats so far—he was interested and interesting... certainly not the flashy ex TV star she'd imagined.

Sebastian was absently tapping a pen against the side of his black-rimmed glasses...clearly thinking. 'Have you considered a general lift instead of going under more knives?'

Their patient was a fifty-seven-year-old California-based criminal lawyer called Tilda Holt. She'd lost over one hundred pounds and needed some help smoothing things over. Tilda didn't like what she called her 'bingo wings', and even though she was already booked for a brachioplasty she was intrigued by the work other people were having done on the premises and had come to find out more.

'Can he give me a face that reflects my young soul, do you think, Dr Ricci? Or is that too much work?' Tilda was looking directly at Mila now.

'Dr Becker's work is some of the best I've seen,' she said tactfully. 'I think you can count yourself lucky you found your way here. How did you hear about Dr Becker's work, can I ask?'

Tilda was back to looking at him in admiration. 'I saw him on the television. I said to my husband, That's the guy for me. He can help me.' She took Sebastian's hand in hers across the table. 'You always had a way of really *seeing* people, Dr Becker, that's why people loved you on that show.'

Mila caught the flicker of embarrassment in Sebastian's eyes as he looked at her over his glasses. She smiled at him. She couldn't help a flutter of affection.

She'd noticed how he gave every consultation himself—in person or via video call. He went to the mainland a lot, too, for people who couldn't travel this far. He wanted to know everyone who walked through his door.

He must know his personality still counted for a lot, she thought, no matter how he appeared to dislike his own celebrity label. And he allowed these patients in, along with their money, because it was helping the island.

Sebastian was leafing through a brochure with Tilda. 'No filters necessary on your photos after this particular procedure. At least, I don't think so. How it works is we fire ultrasound energy into the muscles you'd usually get tightened in a face lift…here, here, here…so no knives and no needles.'

'No knives?'

'Absolutely zero. We get new collagen forming under smoother, brighter skin. Sometimes the cheekbones look more sculpted and defined. I had a patient last month email me to say she hadn't enjoyed wearing make-up for twenty years until she had this procedure.'

Tilda let out a groan. 'I used to love make-up.'

It amused Mila, the way Sebastian could turn these procedures into scenarios that sounded almost exciting. He knew just how to keep a patient's attention—maybe he'd honed that skill on television.

She'd been expecting to find this man a bit spoilt—arrogant, maybe, even flashy. She'd thought maybe he'd come with all the trimmings of a reality TV star. But he was none of those things, from what she'd seen so far. She thought of Annabel and wondered if her sister had felt this same attraction to him when they'd shared their brief encounter.

At the bar she hadn't asked him about what had happened between them. It had been too much even to think about it at the time, reminding her of Annabel and the accident.

There hadn't been time to talk privately since then either. Too many meetings, introductory briefings and shadowing surgical procedures. And in between all that calming breaks spent sipping green tea out in the sun with the staff.

It was beautiful here, and the patients were appreciative and relaxed after their treatments. It was everything she'd hoped for when she'd boarded that plane at a blustery Gatwick Airport. But it was a little unnerving that she was thinking so much about Dr Becker when he wasn't there—especially as he'd only been completely professional with her.

'So, these muscles come up here, and the brow comes up here, and the whole face and neck treatment takes about thirty minutes. It'll cost you less than surgery—a lot less.' Sebastian was back in his swivel chair. He was wearing blue sneakers with jeans under his white coat: trademark Chicago boy.

'Would *you* do it?' Ms Holt asked Mila.

'Only you can decide if you want this procedure, Ms Holt,' she said, blinking herself back to the moment, 'But I can assure you if you choose to do so you'll be in good hands.

'What happened to your arms, Dr Ricci?'

Tilda's question came out of the blue. The woman was studying her scars over the frangipani flowers and candles. Mila felt obliged to leave her wrists facing up on the desk, so Ms Holt could see them. It wasn't the first time she'd been asked about her scars.

'It was an accident,' she said simply. 'I don't really notice them now.'

OK, so that last part was a lie.

Tilda looked sympathetically at Mila. 'Can't you fix them? Someone like you? Can't *yo*u fix them, Dr Becker?'

Sebastian coughed and stepped in quickly, before Mila could even answer. 'I'm afraid our appointment's almost over, Ms Holt. I'd just like to add that with the ultrasound treatment there's no downtime at all—not like with surgery. You'll just look a little suntanned for an hour or so. But that's nothing new around here. We'll let you think about it.'

He stood and ushered her politely towards the door, talking about seeing her on the MAC's private beach in a few days' time for the sea turtle sanctuary fundraiser.

Why did he have to step in? Mila thought in annoyance. He wasn't her protector. She didn't need one.

She'd earned her high position in combat support hospitals, where she'd trained medics on the military camp in spite of her age. She'd even taught a fresh medical team to handle trauma victims her first time in command. In fact, she had excelled at everything she'd ever done—without any guy stepping in on her behalf.

Maybe she was being unfair... He probably assumed she was embarrassed whenever someone mentioned her scars because she hadn't elaborated on how she'd got them. Men often thought they had to protect her because of what she'd been through.

'So...'

Sebastian turned to her when Tilda Holt had gone. Sunlight was streaming from the window across the polished floor onto his sneakers. She was still a little annoyed with him...but he looked really, really good in those glasses.

For a second she thought he was going to come right out and ask her again how she'd got her scars. He must have been wondering ever since he'd first seen them, back when he'd thought she was Annabel. He probably thought she'd got them out on deployment—most people did. Would he ever imagine she'd got them trying to pull her twin sister through a smashed-in car windscreen?

She felt sick even thinking about it. She didn't want him to imagine that. He had his own clear picture of Annabel, whatever that entailed. She wouldn't ruin a nice image of her beautiful sister for anyone.

'Will we see *you* at Friday's fundraiser, Mila? We've got some pretty fun live music lined up. And the turtles could do with your help.'

She caught herself. 'Friday?'

'Yes—you didn't forget about it, did you?'

She wasn't about to tell him, but she *had* totally forgotten.

Sebastian's phone was buzzing on the desk. His brother's name flashed on the screen before he swiped up. 'If you'll excuse me?'

'Jared? Your brother?' she said, remembering how he'd never been to visit—if indeed that rumour was true.

'More like my nephew Charlie on Jared's

phone.' He touched his hand lightly to her shoulder. 'I really do have to take this. It's his birthday and he needs to tell me all about his presents—you know how it is.'

He left the room, chatting to his nephew in an excited voice she knew he probably reserved only for him, and Mila felt her unfortunate soft spot for her current employer soften just a bit more.

'When he gives you that look you can see in that moment *exactly* what millions of viewers saw, watching Dr Sebastian Becker on television,' Rachel sighed. 'Do you know the look I mean? You've seen it, haven't you?'

Sebastian stopped in the shadows at the sound of his name. He couldn't see their faces, and they couldn't see him. But Rachel was what he would call *swooning*. Mila was saying nothing.

'Watch out, Dr Ricci! The Becker boys can change your face and steal your heart,' Rachel enthused, gesturing to Mila's heart with a glass of wine.

They were at the turtle fundraiser, standing on the MAC's beach in the light of a flaming torch stuck in the sand.

'What did I steal?' Sebastian knew his voice would make them both turn around.

'Oh, God.' Rachel covered her face with her hands. 'I'm sorry,' she mumbled through her fingers.

Mila was biting back a smile.

'It's OK, I promise not to steal your heart, Rachel,' he teased, but he couldn't help his eyes lingering on Mila and her curves in a blue dress which swooped at the back in a low V.

'I should go and check on the turtle cake,' Rachel muttered, gathering up her skirt to walk hurriedly in the direction he'd come from.

In the next moment it was just Mila in that dress, and him, and the buzz of the fundraising crowd behind them.

'Catching up on the island gossip, are you?' he asked pointedly. 'I thought you weren't into that.'

'I think Rachel likes to talk.' Mila shot him a sideways glance. 'I was put in an involuntary listening position.'

He swiped up a seashell and led them both down the beach, turning to look over his shoulder and see Rachel watching them from the buffet table.

'She told me she watched every single episode of *Faces of Chicago* before applying to the MAC—all in the name of research,' he disclosed.

'Of *course* for research,' Mila replied, a smile playing on her lips.

She waded out a foot away from him into the shallows, bunching up her dress. He watched the breeze playing with her hair and the silky blue fabric as she inhaled long and deep with her face to the sky. She looked as if she was breathing in life from the water. He wondered if she'd ever been diving.

'So, I heard your big speech earlier,' she said, when she had taken her moment. 'You've been raising tiny turtles till they're big enough to thrive around the coral which you are regenerating with electromagnetic technology? Is that right?'

Her accent was so great when she said, *'Is that right?'* He liked a British accent. Annabel's had been the same, but again it struck him how Annabel had been so very different from Mila.

'That's correct. We're hoping for seventy per cent regeneration in the areas where we've invested. It's early days yet, but we'll keep on monitoring it.'

'Is there *anything* on this island you're not involved in?' she teased, wading with him towards a wooden swing.

'Maybe a couple things,' he consented. 'There's always something to do.'

He held the swing so she could sit on the polished driftwood—and so he'd be able to admire the slope of her shoulders and the backless cut of her dress from behind when he pushed her. He had the swing put here—had even done most of the work himself, with a little help from Ketut. He wouldn't tell Mila how he'd sat here most nights before the MAC had even been built, from sunset into dusk, trying to count the reasons not to jump on a plane, to go and look for Klara.

'Most things are a team effort in a place like this,' he told her, pushing her out on the swing and watching her toes skim the surface. 'And it has to start with ocean conservation—that's what keeps us all afloat on this island.'

'No pun intended?'

'None whatsoever.'

He let the waves lap his calves as she dug her feet into the sand again. The wind picked up strands of her hair and they tickled his face as he tightened his fists around the swing's ropes.

'Have you ever been diving, Dr Ricci?' he

asked over her shoulder. Her hair smelled good…
like the incense that swirled on the MAC's reception desk.

'No,' she answered on a breath. 'Not in the
ocean. Describe it. The feeling—not the tech-
nique.'

He considered this. 'It's like a cranial cleanse,'
he said, loosening his fists around the ropes.
'When you're down there it's possible to completely switch your mind off. You have no inter-
nal chatter—nothing pressing, at least. It's just
you and the sound of your own breath in your
ears.'

'It sounds magical. Like the very best kind of
meditation.'

'It is. Close your eyes.'

One strap of her dress tumbled down over
her shoulder in the breeze. She left it there and
obeyed him.

You're drifting with the current,' he told her.
'Like you're breathing with the earth itself. In.
Out. In. Out. You don't need your hands much,
just your eyes, and it's all about controlling your
breathing.'

'You're really selling this to me,' she said after
a moment.

Her eyes were still closed and her head was tilted back slightly, almost against him, not quite touching.

'Maybe I'll try it…'

'I'll take you,' he told her. It surprised him how much he wanted to show Mila Ricci all the things he loved most about the ocean. 'I can't believe in all your Army training, you never went scuba diving.'

'I did dive a couple of times in a lake, but I was always too busy up on the surface throwing hand grenades to put it into practice in the ocean.'

She was smiling as she turned the swing around to face him, making the ropes twist tightly above her. Her bare legs were locked between his for a second, or maybe he pulled her there…he wasn't sure…

'Hello? Dr Becker! Hello!'

A man with blue hair was waving a coconut at them from the shoreline.

Sebastian released the swing's ropes and Mila was almost thankful for the interruption. Sebastian had placed her under some kind of spell and she'd been momentarily transfixed by what he was saying and his presence in general.

She was supposed to be shaking off this attraction to him—they had to work together. Not to mention his previous...whatever it had been...with Annabel. But it was pretty hard to stay away when he had that...*thing*... Rachel had been talking about. Magnetic appeal.

The man with blue hair greeted Sebastian with what she could only describe as reverence and seemed not even to notice her presence. She recognised him from the patient files: Hugo O'Shea. He must have just arrived for his treatment. She believed it was a routine penis enlargement.

According to Rachel, the man was a renowned internet gossip queen. 'He loves gossip more than I do,' she'd told Mila, which Mila found hard to believe.

Hugo's board shorts were a patchwork of colourful bananas. 'Beautiful evening! I'm sure the turtles are as grateful for your work as I am, Dr Becker.' He raised an eyebrow at Mila.

'Apologies, Hugo, this is Dr Mila Ricci,' Sebastian said smoothly. 'She'll be with you during your surgery.'

Hugo swivelled his entire body towards her, extending a hand with a flourish. 'I don't mind a woman's touch,' he said as she shook it. 'But I think we both prefer Dr Becker's—am I right?'

He winked and leaned into her, fanning his face.

Mila smiled politely.

'Can I get a photo of you both? Just the one? The moon behind you is perfect.'

'No, not tonight,' Sebastian said curtly, before she could reply, and turned to leave. 'Enjoy your night, Hugo.'

Mila considered letting Sebastian go alone, and ending their conversation entirely, but she realised she wasn't done yet. She shouldn't let a pushy patient come between them—that much she knew—but it was something else that spurred her legs into action and made her follow him away from the crowd, up the rocks to the viewpoint.

This side of the island was quieter. The waves lapped at the rocks with big, loud sloshes and ahead the black night sea was like a blanket rolled out by the mountains in the distance.

'You really don't like anyone taking your photo, do you?' she said cautiously, lowering herself to the sandy rocks beside him. Up here, they were safe from prying eyes on the beach. She knew that was what he was most afraid of.

'O'Shea signed an NDA,' Sebastian said. 'He knows we don't let cameras in the MAC.'

Mila pulled her knees to her chest. 'Is this about what happened in Chicago?' she probed gently. 'I know you were stalked by the paparazzi. But I don't know the exact details...'

'They followed me and Klara everywhere—relentlessly,' he told her. His jaw was clenched now, his shoulders stiff and tense, as if even the memory was painful to contain. 'They caught her getting out of the car once, outside the Valentine's Gala on Lakeshore Drive. It was windy, and Klara's dress was—unfortunately—blown into a highly compromising position. The paps were all over it: zooming in, pointing out all the things you wouldn't want anyone pointing out. You haven't heard all this from anyone else?'

Mila put a hand to her mouth, shaking her head. The humiliation. She couldn't bear it. The poor woman...

'It was the worst possible outcome for a kindergarten teacher,' he continued.

'She was a teacher?'

'We were different,' he admitted. '*Very* different. I guess I liked it that she wasn't part of my world. I met her through my nephew Charlie. I went to collect him from school one day. Klara was there, stacking all these tiny plastic chairs...'

He trailed off, as though he realised he was telling her too much.

'Some of the kids' parents got together...made a huge deal out of the photo,' he said. 'They made out she was unfit to be around their kids. She *loved* those kids,' he stressed. 'They were her whole world. She was devastated. Then one publication...' he paused to sit up and make quotation marks with his fingers '"...*revealed*" that she was seeing another guy, which made it worse. He was a colleague—the principal of the kindergarten—but they printed photos of them talking outside the school. His wife got all suspicious, and then she was dragged into it...'

'This is horrifying!' said Mila.

He nodded slowly, his eyes on a night dive boat chugging out into the blackness.

'The principal offered her a sabbatical, to get away from it all. I quit the show. I thought maybe I'd go away with her, but she wanted to go alone. She got a volunteer position at some school in Thailand, deleted all her social media accounts, changed her number… She wouldn't even see me before she left.'

Mila pulled her eyes away from his biceps as he leaned back on his elbows with his face to the sky. 'Not at all?'

'Not even to say goodbye. I guess she thought I might show up with a bunch of photographers behind me. I couldn't really blame her.'

'But you had no closure?'

She realised this was probably getting far too personal now, but she couldn't help wanting to know. She would rather hear the truth from him than some rehashed version of the story on the rumour mill.

Mila remembered now how Rachel had told her he'd used to fly from Bali every weekend to try and find Klara. She didn't ask if it was true, and Sebastian didn't mention it, but the look on his face told her that he must have really loved this woman.

She felt a flicker of envy strike unannounced at the thought. She hadn't ever loved anyone like that—she might not *ever* love anyone like that.

'I guess I found closure here,' he said. 'I brought a skeleton team out with me and we worked bit by bit on renovations at the Blue Ray while the MAC was being built. I signed up to teach people to dive, set up the turtle foundation with Neesha and her husband—you'll meet them later—and spent a lot of time just getting to know the locals. That's important in a place like this. We had to ease our way in slowly on the island...build the trust. Then we opened the doors to the MAC and it's been non-stop since then, pretty much.'

'And what about the show? What happened when you quit?'

Sebastian bristled, once again examining the distant fishing boats. 'I half expected Jared to call it quits too, and follow me out here. He saw what I went through with Klara, and he knew they could have done the same to him and Laura—that's his wife.'

'Why didn't they?'

He shrugged. 'They were married, they were stable—influencers for the perfect family life. Laura has a cooking blog and she does a podcast for mums. Maybe that's not so titillating for readers? I don't know. You can't tell who they'll make their next target, or what lies they'll choose to spread, but I guess they chose me and Klara because we were younger, we went out more—

we gave them more chances to pair their head-line-grabbing stories with photos. They took *so many* photos!'

Mila was shaking her head, still hugging her knees. This was all news to her, and she wondered what it must have been like for him and Klara, living in the eye of a media storm. She supposed it wasn't dissimilar to being in Afghanistan in some ways—living in fear, priming herself for things that might not even happen.

'The network wanted to try another season,' he continued. 'They found a replacement surgeon, so Jared wouldn't have to, and threw more money at us. They basically made it impossible for him to leave. The show took off again without me, and Chicago's media found something else to do instead of ramming their camera lenses into my business. Life goes on.'

He tossed a pebble over the rocks, dragged a hand through his hair and shot her a sheepish smile.

'I don't know why I'm boring you with all this, Mila. It's not exactly a life-threatening issue.'

'You're not boring me. It's nice to get to know you,' she said truthfully. 'The man behind the surgical mask.'

She watched the way his shoulders relaxed suddenly, as if in relief.

'What does the future hold for you, then?' she pressed. 'Do you want to stay here for ever? Don't you want a family of your own?'

He turned to her. 'Why can't I do that here?'

Mila paused. For some reason she hadn't expected that. 'I can imagine there would be a lot to inspire kids growing up here...' she told him carefully, and realised she was picturing it herself now.

A future here, teaching kids how to love the ocean, seeing them running around the island barefoot, taking reading classes on the sand... That all seemed pretty good to her, even though she'd decided a long time ago that she was never having children.

'There would be worse places to raise a family, don't you think?' he asked.

'I don't know... I don't really think about raising a family anywhere.'

He studied her with interest for a moment. She was ashamed to admit it, but she was afraid to have a child herself. What if she lost it or something happened to it...? Or what if something happened to the father? She couldn't bear the thought of enduring that kind of emotional loss a second time round.

'Well, I'd rather do it here than in Chicago,' he told her. 'I'm not saying I never go back there to visit—in fact I'm heading back soon for my mother's birthday. But, between you and me, I never wanted to do that show in the first place. The further I am away from all that now, the better.'

Sebastian's shirt was open…four, maybe five buttons. It was the most she'd seen of him outside his scrubs since the last time they'd talked properly, like this. The breeze was teasing his thick brown hair and she wondered momentarily what it might be like to touch it.

'Why did you do the show then?' she asked.

'Mom wanted it—she thought it was something that our father would have done if he'd still been here. Jared wasn't sure, but he saw the potential for attracting new clients. It was closer to home than my idea anyway…which was to set up this place here.'

He gestured around them.

'This place was always my passion—not theirs. It was on hold for a long time while the show was taking up all my time. I wanted to quit as soon as they started sensationalising everything. We all knew Dad wouldn't have wanted *that* kind of attention on the institute—all those cameras that never turned off, the ones that started following me and Klara home. But it took that photo getting out for me to quit for good. Maybe Klara thought I'd quit too late.'

He picked up a stone and smoothed it between his fingers.

'She wouldn't have wanted to stay here anyway. She was always a city girl, really. And I guess this place was always going to steal me away, sooner or later. I mean—look at it.'

He gestured at the sweeping ocean ahead of him, then turned to offer her his full attention.

'When are we going to find the time to take you on your first ocean dive, huh?'

Mila took the opportunity he was giving her to change the topic, and soon they'd both lost track of time talking about manta rays and shipwrecks, and Charlie's school projects, and their very different school days, their very different preferences in clothing back in the nineties, when they'd taken their boards for Surgical Critical Care certification…and how they'd both somehow grown up having never seen *Star Wars*.

Sometimes Mila saw Annabel in her mind's eye, sitting there with them on the lookout, daring her to ask Sebastian what had happened between them when she was here.

Why couldn't she do it?

Mila knew why. She just found it hard to admit. It was the same reason something prickled inside her when he spoke about his past with Klara.

She was starting to really like this man. And it frightened her.

CHAPTER FOUR

'YOUNG GIRL, EIGHT years old.' Dr Fatema Halabi looked harried. 'We're vaccinating for rabies, but she's going to need more than a few stitches. We brought her straight here from the Blue Ray.'

Dr Halabi was a new recruit on the MAC's medical residency training programme. She'd done three years of general surgery in a practice in Charlotte, North Carolina, and now she was filling in with general duties around her plastic surgery training under Dr Becker's guidance.

She'd wheeled this patient into the light, airy, jasmine-scented treatment room before Mila had even pulled on her gloves. The unfortunate dog-bite victim was a French tourist—Francoise Marchand. Her mother was close behind.

Mila peeled back the huge bandage that was struggling to soak up the blood and surveyed the damage. She saw immediately the lacerations to the child's nose and lips. It looked pretty bad, but not as bad as she'd anticipated...considering the last dog bite she'd had to treat.

'How big was the dog that bit you?' she asked the little girl.

'It was some kind of Alsatian—big, very huge!' her mother cut in, in broken English. Her chin wobbled, as if she was struggling not to cry as Fatema applied fresh cloths to the wound. 'The crazy dog! It was lunging at her! It should have been tied up! What is wrong with this place? It's just not safe for children here...'

'Mrs Marchand, I can assure you the island *is* safe,' Mila informed her, wondering if the statement was indeed correct. 'The dog *should* have been tied up, I agree, but we're here now. We're going to help Francoise, OK?'

Francoise sniffled, watching Fatema, who was the picture of calm. Mila knew she had to stay the same—as much for this mother as for her child, who was still conscious and in pain. Francoise's long blonde hair was matted with blood. So was her watermelon-patterned T-shirt. She was being braver than her mother, though.

'Francoise didn't m-mean to upset the d-dog,' Mrs Marchand stammered, clutching the side of the bed. 'She was just trying to get to the puppies. The mother dog must have thought she was too close… She just went for her… There was nothing I could do… This island is *not* safe!'

Mila put a hand to her shoulder and led her to the leather chair in a corner of the spacious room. It all made sense now, she thought with a frown. Approaching a mother dog and her new puppies without the owner's consent was never a good idea. This might have happened anywhere.

'This is not your fault, OK?' she said, although it wasn't true. 'I need you to stay calm, for Francoise's sake.'

The frazzled-looking woman swiped at her watery blue eyes. Mila knew it was imperative she stay calm. Her daughter was absorbing her panic like a sponge and amplifying it.

'Maybe you'd like to wait outside? We'll come and get you when we're done.'

Mila walked Mrs Marchand to the door. She needed to focus. The periorbital oedema was obvious around the girl's left eye—severe bruising that must have come from her struggles. She'd noticed lacerations to the soft tissue around her upper lip too, and to the skin across the lower left jawbone. Hopefully there wouldn't be any nerve damage.

Fatema excused herself and Rachel ran the X-rays.

Mila found she was waiting for Sebastian. His trademark treatment would be needed here. The new revolutionary thread dissolved faster in the skin, meaning there was no need for removal and less visible scarring on the lips, face, or mouth. Francoise and her mother likely didn't know how lucky they were that this had happened here. Not that she should be using the word *lucky*, really.

'You're being so brave,' she soothed Francoise, and the kid almost smiled—before wincing again in pain. She was handling the injections and the clean-up well, thank goodness.

Mila knew that dog bites accounted for thousands of facial injuries every year, and that over half the victims were children. She'd seen a few dogs around the island. She'd never thought to fear them.

She studied the X-rays on the computer monitor, but she couldn't help the flashbacks. Last time she'd dealt with a dog-bite it had been even worse than this. The German Shepherd had been terrified when they'd found it. It had been chained to a fence at a tiny military outpost. His paw had been a bloody mess, slit by razor wire.

He'd lunged as they'd approached the body of his owner—an Afghan officer who'd been shot in the back. She could still see his face, and the dog, too. The poor thing must have been there a while, listening to the blasts and seeing the shrapnel raining down, watching his owner lose his fight for life just feet away. No wonder it had launched itself at them and almost torn her colleague Neil's face off.

'Are you OK?'

Mila looked up from the screen with a start. Sebastian was looking at her strangely. She hadn't heard him come in. He was clean-shaven, wearing a red shirt and jeans with black sneakers.

'I'm fine,' she answered, though she knew her heart had sped up.

He pulled on a white coat and she caught a whiff of sunscreen and a new cologne she'd never smelled on him before. She briefed him quickly on the situation, noting how her palms were clammier than they had been before he'd walked in.

She resented this sudden rush of nerves at performing the revolutionary treatment Dr Becker had perfected. This would be her first time using the lasers, but it was him more than the notion of performing that unsettled her.

'I have it under control,' she told him, looking him square in the eyes.

Of course Mila was in full control. But Sebastian kept throwing her speculative looks, as if he was monitoring her mood as well as her capabilities.

An ER doctor over at the Blue Ray could stitch up a wound, maybe even conceal it pretty well, but it took a surgeon's work to stop a person living with noticeable scars for the rest of their life. She had to block him out—or at least pretend she wasn't so damn attracted to the man that she physically felt his eyes on her wherever she moved in the room.

Mila woke with a jump. 'No, no, no…' she muttered to herself, reaching for her phone. It was only midnight, but she'd had the dream again. She knew she wouldn't be able to get back to sleep now.

Flustered, she lay back down under the fan, trying to let the cooling air work its magic, but images were coursing through her brain at a million miles an hour, as usual.

She squeezed her eyes shut. No, she couldn't bear it any longer.

Wearily she threw back the cotton sheets, splashed some cool water on her face in the bathroom. Looking at herself in the mirror, she let out a long sigh. *Why* was she still having the dream?

She pulled on a dress over her underwear and stepped out onto the porch. The moon and the stars were bright above the waving palm trees. She considered lying in the hammock there, trying to go back to sleep out there in the safe confines of the MAC's staff quarters. But maybe a short walk would clear her head.

She slipped into her sandals and set off into the warm, muggy night, taking the path around the MAC's grounds.

The dream played on in her head, no matter how she tried to block it by appreciating the island scenery. It never got boring to her—the mountains glowing in the moonlight, the twinkling lights on the bobbing boats, the gentle lap of the waves on the shore. But the dream was a nightmare every time. It threw her right back to the night of the accident. There was Annabel, slumped over the steering wheel.

Mila stopped at the swing in the water, settled on the heart-shaped seat. She couldn't even stop the dream invading her memories now that she was awake.

In reality, on the night it had happened, Mila had known she was going to be too late to help her twin the second she'd seen her—maybe even before that. She'd sensed it somehow…the lack, the loss. Maybe that was why all her years of training had flown out the window and she'd frozen.

But in her dream Annabel's car was in Afghanistan, not rural England. Mila was heaving her out through the windscreen on her own, just as she had in real life. Rocket-propelled grenades blasted all around them. Fire blazed and flames lapped the blown-out windows of a tall building. Women were screaming in the dust from the fallout, staggering over to her with their wounded children, begging for help.

Mila couldn't save Annabel and she couldn't save anyone else either. It was stress, grief, guilt—all of it tangled up in one dream. She'd had it over and over again since she'd arrived here on the island.

The ocean helped a little, she thought, letting

the ripples wash over her ankles. Maybe going on a dive with Sebastian would help even more. He seemed to think diving was like switching your brain off for a while. She could do with some of that. They hadn't managed to squeeze it in yet, though—they'd just been too busy.

Mila was walking back towards her room, thinking of Sebastian, when the sound of the dog barking close by made her jump. She was probably on edge, after what had happened to Francoise, but she hurried on, back towards the staff quarters, hoping it wasn't the same dog that had bitten the child.

Hadn't Sebastian said that someone had re-moved the animal and her pups and put them somewhere safe?

It couldn't be the same one, she thought. But it didn't stop a spike of adrenaline flooding her veins anyway.

The barking tore up the night again. At first she couldn't see a dog. Then it appeared on the sandy path, right in front of her. Mila stopped in her tracks. There was no one else around. The dog was big and stocky, speckled with black and white spots. It was staring straight at her, not barking any more, just looking at her inquisitively.

She took a tentative step towards it, taking a calm approach. 'Are you lost, buddy?' she asked softly. His tail was the longest she had ever seen. This was a real Bali Dog, she observed, wondering if it was friendly or not.

'Bruno!'

Mila spun around at the voice.

Sebastian was sprinting towards them. The dog met him in the middle of the path, jumping up at the Chicago Cubs sports shirt he was wearing, pressing his big paws against his chest. Sebastian was wearing board shorts and flip-flops too, looking the most casual she had seen him since the day they'd met. She couldn't help running her eyes up and down his body.

'Hey, Mila… Sorry, did he scare you? He got out through the gates—someone must have left them open by mistake.'

Someone?

'This is your dog?'

Mila smoothed down her dress, embarrassed suddenly by her un-brushed hair and just-out-of-bed look. She hadn't even cleaned her teeth. She watched Sebastian crouch to the ground and ruffle the big dog's fur lovingly. The dog re-paid him by licking his cheek, arms and neck... everywhere he could reach.

'He's only with me till we find him a new home,' he disclosed, laughing at the dog's enthusiasm. 'Mila, meet Bruno. Bruno is...a handful. He wouldn't hurt anyone, though, if you were worried...?'

'I wasn't,' she said, maybe too quickly. 'What are you doing up so late?'

He stood up straight, fixed her with a piercing gaze. Damn him for looking so good—even at midnight.

'I could ask you the same thing,' he said.

'I couldn't sleep,' she confessed.

'Something on your mind?'

She nodded, and walked with him along the path, past the swaying palms. The sea was still swooshing behind them. His private home was only metres away, but she realised she had never seen beyond the tall wooden gates before. He kept them locked, as if his house was like some kind of ivory tower. Knowing a little about his past with the paps, she could understand why.

They stopped when they got to the now open gates. Bruno charged back inside and Mila caught a glimpse of Sebastian's place for the first time. Modest. Small. One level. No swimming pool. Nothing like what she'd been expecting. She'd thought it would be something more extravagant, reflective of his fortune, maybe.

He put his hand to her arm gently, looking at her in concern. 'You looked like you had something on your mind today, when that kid with the dog bite came in. Are you OK? We're not overworking you, are we?'

'No, Sebastian, I'm used to hard work.'

'Well, I *know* that.'

She looked down at his hand on her bare arm. The warmth of it flooded through her, and with it came a surge of emotion that threatened to turn into tears. She swallowed it back, looking away.

'It's just…sometimes I dream about her, you know… Annabel. It's the anniversary of her death, soon. I guess she's just been on my mind more often than usual. Don't worry, it won't affect my work. I hope it hasn't—'

'Hey.'

He caught her chin for a second, guiding her eyes to his. His features wore a look of pure concern now. She felt her lungs tighten and her breath catch.

'Mila, your work is not what I'm worried about.'

She fought not to let those tears spring from her eyes. She shouldn't have told him about the anniversary—it was way too personal. But it had just slipped out. She was so exhausted and his kindness was killing her.

'I want you to be happy here,' he added.

He looked as though her happiness was genuinely important to him. Mila's heart swelled just a little bit more.

'I love it here,' she told him honestly, pulling her eyes away. 'It's everything Annabel said it was. Better.'

For a moment she considered asking him what had happened between her sister and him. She should just ask him, so she could let it go either way. But it made her feel like a paranoid teenager, which was certainly not the impression she wanted to give him. Whenever she plucked up the courage to ask whether he and her twin had been intimate or not, the thought of the ensuing conversation, focused on Annabel and the way she'd died…because *she'd* been too frozen to help her…was just too much. She couldn't do it—not yet.

Behind him she could just make out the living room of his place. The decidedly non-ostentatious, cosy-looking room was lit up softly and the door was open, as if he'd left in a hurry to chase the dog. The huge window revealed some gym equipment, a black sofa, and a coffee table with a bottle of wine on it.

She could see two wine glasses, both empty. Her stomach started churning.

Had he been drinking with the same 'someone' who'd left the gates open?

'Do you want to come in? I have some tea…' Sebastian paused, looked a little sheepish, as if maybe he knew it wasn't very professional to be asking her that.

But now she just couldn't help wondering who'd been drinking wine with him so close to midnight. She felt him watching her, seeing her looking at his lit-up living room and the wine glasses. Embarrassment flushed her cheeks.

Why did she care if he'd had a guest over?

'I should probably be getting back,' she told him, hoping he wouldn't see how this was affecting her. 'See you at the MAC. Goodnight, Sebastian.'

CHAPTER FIVE

'HE WAS ADVISED against XXL, so he's going for extra-large,' Dr Halabi confirmed out loud, reading from the notes on the monitor.

Sebastian winked at his resident trainee. 'Extra-large is enough for this guy. If he had XXL he'd fall over,' he said, and Fatema giggled.

Hugo O'Shea was almost under. His eyelids were fluttering. His blue hair seemed even bluer in the surgery lights. The long, slick piece of silicone they'd insert into Hugo's currently not so prized manhood floated promisingly in a beaker of antibiotic solution next to them.

Sebastian had done this procedure hundreds of times—on and off camera, he thought wryly. He'd done it so much he could probably do it with his eyes closed, but he still loved teaching others these skills. Fatema was a keen student. Soon she'd be doing the routine procedures herself, while he got back to scar repairs with Mila...

and the million other things that demanded his attention.

There was a knock on the door. Mila stepped in.

'Sorry to interrupt, Doctor,' she said. 'Is it OK if I grab that light?' She motioned to the mobile surgery light in the corner.

'Of course, Dr Ricci.'

He let his eyes linger on her bare ankles as she crossed the floor in her white sneakers. She was wearing her brown hair in a bun, pinned to the top of her head. It reminded him of Annabel for a second. Annabel had worn her hair like that...he was sure of it. Sometimes it still blew his mind that he'd met Mila's twin first, but the two were completely different women in his mind. They looked alike, but that was all.

Mila was an entirely new species.

He still couldn't figure her out.

He hadn't seen her outside of the MAC for the last few days. The last time they'd spoken without other people around had been outside his house in the middle of the night, after she'd come across Bruno. He'd asked her inside, but she'd hurried off. He assumed he'd made her feel a little awkward. They were colleagues after all—

and he never invited colleagues from the MAC home, nor patients.

He'd realised when he'd gone back inside and seen the wine glasses on the table that she'd probably seen them too, and had maybe thought he'd been entertaining a woman.

Not this time. It had been just Neesha and her husband Dan—his friends from the turtle sanctuary. They'd been adding up the profits from the fundraiser and planning where the money should go, along with a little extra donation from his own private funds for some new tanks for the baby turtles. Neesha had poured wine for herself and Dan. He'd had a herbal tea himself.

In one way he liked it that seeing those wine glasses might have evoked a stab of jealousy in Mila; it wasn't as if he hadn't been admiring her work…and her eyes…and her body…but in another way he couldn't deny that he was concerned for her.

She clearly thought about Annabel a lot more than he did, and more often than she was letting on. Coming here was reminding her of her twin—especially because he'd met her here, too. He knew how grief could flare up when you least wanted it to. He'd been through it after his father died.

Mila went to leave the room with the light she'd come in for, without looking his way.

'See you later?' he asked her as she reached for the door.

She turned back to him and he saw Fatema glance up at them over Hugo.

He cleared his throat, hoping Mila hadn't forgotten. 'The dive centre this afternoon?'

It had taken ages to get a slot when both of them were free.

Mila blinked. Her phone buzzed in her pocket. Distracted, she fished it out as she said, 'Yes, Doctor... Sorry for disturbing you—excuse me.' And she left the room.

When she'd left, Fatema couldn't get her words out fast enough. 'Diving? You and Dr Ricci? Better not tell Rachel about that. She likes to pair people up, and I think you're both on her hit list. Young, single, beautiful, tortured... It's like you belong together. Sorry, Doctor, am I speaking out of line?'

Fatema flushed a little at the realisation that she had just called him beautiful and tortured. Sebastian fought to stop the amusement from showing on his face; he'd been called worse things in his time on the show.

'Shall we begin?' he suggested.

His afternoon off couldn't get here fast enough.

'How's it going over there? It's been a while since I've spoken to you...'

'Sorry, Mum,' Mila said, sinking down onto the low stone wall outside the MAC and observing the patients lying around, reading or chattering in the grounds. 'The time difference here is crazy—plus we've been so busy.'

She heard her mum let out a sigh down the phone. 'I figured as much. I won't keep you.'

'No, no, it's OK. I have a few minutes. Dr Becker is training someone at the moment, and then we're in for a scar repair. It really is non-stop around here, but I'm sorry I haven't called you as much I should.'

'I don't expect you to, darling. I'm fine over here.'

Mila wasn't so sure. Her mother had a way of putting on a brave face. 'Are you really fine? What have you been doing?'

Her mum paused. 'This and that. I watched a couple of episodes of that show your famous doctor used to be in. *Faces of Chicago*. Is he married?'

Mila shook her head at the sandy ground. Trust her mum to ask that. 'No, he's not married.'

She pictured Sebastian a few nights ago, outside his house, all smiles and moonlit muscles and charm. She was still so embarrassed at having shown her weaknesses around him. She knew she'd appeared overly emotional, telling him about her dreams and then hurrying off after seeing those wine glasses. The man was entitled to entertain whoever he wanted. He must think she was crazy.

She'd been so mortified about it she'd been keeping away from him whenever possible. She wasn't used to men stirring up her emotions. It made her feel far too vulnerable for her own liking. Besides, she wasn't here for *him*, technically speaking.

'Well, I was just calling to say I've posted you a letter,' her mum said.

'A letter? That's delightfully old-school of you, Mum. What's in it?'

'It's just a few photos. I found them in Annabel's drawer. I thought you might like to have them over there with you as keepsakes.'

Mila's throat felt tight. 'You were looking through Annabel's drawers?'

'I... I was missing her. And you. I think I needed to do it.'

'Oh, Mum.'

Mila could picture her mother at home, curled up with her legs under her at her usual end of the sofa, a book on the arm. Maybe a cup of her favourite tea. They had both cried together on that sofa for days after Annabel had—

No. She couldn't think about it again. She felt guilty for being so far away. And now her mother had started going through Annabel's things without her.

'I saw someone else wearing her clothes the other day,' her mother continued. 'That yellow dress with the black spots—remember it? The one she ordered from the Japanese warehouse?'

Mila swallowed. 'I remember.'

'Annabel loved that dress.'

'I know, Mum.'

She and her mother had made the mistake of taking some of Annabel's clothes and shoes to the local charity shop a few months after the accident. Their good deed—intended as a method of coping with their grief—had backfired badly when they'd started seeing women around the town wearing the donated clothes. Her mother had come home in tears several times, thinking she'd just seen Annabel.

After that neither of them had been able to bear to go back to her things. There were boxes and drawers of her personal items that hadn't been touched since.

'Let me know when the letter arrives,' her mum said. 'I don't know how long it will take to reach you out there, but I thought you might appreciate something on the anniversary…you know. You will call me, won't you?'

Mila's heart ached. She fixed her eyes on the ocean. Someone was swinging on the sea swing where Sebastian had first offered to take her diving. 'Of course I'll call you.'

Her mother sounded concerned. 'You won't be alone on the day, will you?'

Mila bit her lip. 'I won't be alone, I promise. *You* won't be alone, will you?'

'I might have company. Either way, I'll keep busy. Maybe your famous doctor can distract you, Is he as good looking as he is on the television?'

She rolled her eyes, smiling now. 'He's an

inspiration, Mum. He's even taking me scuba diving.'

'Really? He dives, too?'

'He pretty much does everything on this island.'

'Did he take Annabel diving? You said before that he met her. I still can't get over that—what a coincidence!'

Mila felt the usual stab of envy, confusion and nausea. She felt it whenever she thought about Sebastian and Annabel together—which was often.

'I don't know, Mum. I haven't asked what they did when Annabel was here. It's none of my business, is it? I have to go. Thank you for sending me the photos. I love you.'

She was determined not to let her emotions overwhelm her with people around, but her mother was still talking.

'When you finish your stint out there and come home we'll go through the rest of her things together, OK? It's time, Mila.'

The coral reefs surrounding the islands were home to some of the planet's most diverse marine life. Sebastian watched Mila admiring the brown and white stripes of a solo lion fish with a look of total awe as he floated beside her.

She'd said she'd done some diving training before, in her Army days, but she'd never been in the ocean. Looking at her now, he couldn't believe it. She exuded confidence—more than many of his other students on their first dives. She'd followed Big Al, one of their rescue turtles for a good ten minutes, and he'd got a little kick out of the way her eyes had lit up just at drifting along, observing his barnacle-speckled shell, his scars and his wise hooded eyes.

Damn, she was beautiful with her hair down... and up.

He usually couldn't remember his thoughts after a dive, but when they finally climbed back onto the boat he realised he'd spent most of the dive both admiring her and worrying about what she might be thinking.

'So, did you switch off completely down there?' he asked, watching her shake out her hair.

He'd reserved the boat just for them, but his buddy and driver Ketut was watching them intently, just like Fatema and Rachel were clearly doing behind their backs. Maybe next time he'd take her out alone.

BECKY WICKS 99

'I don't actually remember.' Mila looked pensive as he placed her heavy tank back in its holder and signalled to Ketut to start the engine. 'But it's true what you said. It's so peaceful down there. I really needed it. Thank you, Sebastian.'

He stepped closer, softly brushed a strand of damp hair back behind her ear. 'You're welcome.'

Ketut cleared his throat at the steering wheel and Mila looked uncomfortable for a second, then broke contact by stepping back.

'That turtle...' she started. 'The big one...'

'Big Al? Yeah, he's a pretty special guy.'

'What happened to him? I saw his fins, with all those scars.'

'He got into a fight with a boat propeller. That's what we think happened anyway.'

'He does look sad,' she mused, following his eyes to the jagged slashes across her left inner forearm. 'But he's so beautiful.'

Sebastian tossed their fins into a box along with the masks and snorkels. 'So are you, in case you ever doubt that. Turn around,' he instructed.

He lifted her wet hair and released the zip of her wetsuit slowly, noting the shape of her shoulders, the contours of her body as he helped to pull it down to her waist. Mila was tense, though.

'I should tell you…that dive was so much more enjoyable than the lake dives we did in training, pulling all those…' She grimaced as she turned around in his arms.

'All those what?' he asked curiously.

'Fake bodies,' she replied. 'They had us helping rescue divers treat the bodies so we'd know how to handle it if it really happened. I don't need to tell you this was a thousand times better.'

He motioned for her to follow him up to the roof of the boat—his favourite place. Her bare midriff was taut and toned. He caught her appraising him too as they stood there on the roof of the bobbing boat.

His hours in the home gym had paid off, he knew that, but Mila had probably always been this way. She'd worked her brain and her body equally in the Army—he had probably only heard about a fraction of the things she'd done and seen. It was eternally fascinating to him. Her scars were beautiful to him. She was beautiful inside and out.

'Maybe next time we'll go to Shark Reef,' he told her, taking a seat on the hot wooden roof and rolling his own wetsuit down to his waist.

'It's a little further out…off the next island. The current has to be just right.'

'I thought you said there aren't any sharks any more?'

He dangled his legs over the side and folded his arms over the railing. Mila's wet hair caught the afternoon sun as she sat beside him. Their bare arms brushed on the hot metal.

'Not many, and it's a gift if you actually get to see one. We donate to the shark nursery off Lombok, so the numbers are rising slowly.'

'Sharks, turtles, dogs, humans…is there anything you're not saving on this island, Dr Becker?'

For the first time in days Mila offered him a real, genuine smile and he felt a weight lift from his shoulders.

'Talking of dogs, thank you for walking Bruno home with me the other night. My friends Neesha and Dan came over—they must have forgotten to shut the gates. They did have a little wine while they were at my place.'

Mila looked indifferent, but he swore he saw her cheeks flush just a little. He didn't have to explain himself—he knew that. He could have anyone he liked over to his house. He could have a woman over if he wanted. But he didn't. Not any more. It surprised him, this need for Mila to know he wasn't playing around.

'You know,' she said, letting out a sigh, 'this is where I first saw you—up here on this roof, the day I arrived. I'd be lying if I told you that you didn't get my attention, looking all…like that.'

She pulled a face and motioned to his bare chest and wet hair, and he laughed.

'Is that so Dr Ricci? Well, I'd be lying if I told you I didn't see you then, too.'

'But you thought I was Annabel.'

Mila rested her head on her arms as he floundered for words.

'It's OK. I wonder what she'd say if she could see us now, working together…diving together.'

'She would probably think it was a pretty funny coincidence. Wouldn't anyone think that?' he asked, slightly annoyed with himself for his initial mistake over her identity. It still bothered him, the way he'd confused the two of them and been so vocal about her changing her name.

'I don't know. I can't speak for my twin. She's not here. I wish she was.'

'When is the anniversary, exactly?' he asked cautiously.

He'd sensed her tense up the second he'd said he thought Annabel would find it amusing, knowing Mila was with him there. He shouldn't have put words in her mouth. It had clearly bothered Mila.

'You mentioned it was coming up to three years since she died?'

She closed her eyes to the sun. 'It's in a few weeks. I might take a day off, if that's OK—do something nice for her. I don't know yet. I haven't had a chance to really think about what I'll do besides call my mother. It's a tough day for her, too.'

'I'm sure. Is she alone over there?'

'You mean, does she have a man? I don't think so. There hasn't really been anyone since she divorced my father. She has a lot of friends, though.'

'I can help you think of something to do here, if you want…to take your mind off it.'

She seemed to contemplate his offer for a moment. 'Thank you. I don't know if *anything* will take my mind off it, but I appreciate that, Sebastian.'

Colleagues or not, the urge to touch her, to reassure her that he was here for her, was overpowering. He couldn't help it. He reached his hand to the back of her head and drew her gently against his shoulder, keeping his hand in her soft damp hair.

They rode back to shore like that, in silence.

Thank goodness it was only a short boat ride back to the beach. Mila could practically feel the sparks flying between them on the roof. It was getting more difficult to ignore their obvious chemistry. Even resting her head on his comforting shoulder felt as if he was rolling out the red carpet, inviting her further in.

What had possessed her to admit she had noticed him on day one, before she'd even got off the boat? She didn't know. But something about his presence was comforting, and real, and he'd seemed to want her to know he hadn't been entertaining anyone in his house lately except friends.

No. She couldn't go there.

Would Annabel really think their meeting was a funny coincidence?

She had asked that very question out loud and sent it off on the wind, many times, longing for an answer. All she'd got in return were more bad dreams that woke her up in a cold sweat.

Sebastian had taken care of returning the dive equipment. It was after four p.m. now, and the afternoon sun cast a flattering light on his biceps as he ordered them both takeaway smoothies at the dive shop bar.

She was trying and failing to find an excuse not to spend the rest of her afternoon with him when a child in blue denim shorts tugged at her shirt from behind. It was Francoise, the French girl who'd come in with the dog bite.

'Hey, you!'

Her mother was hovering at the entrance to the dive shop, waiting for her daughter. They raised their hands at each other from afar.

'I was on my way to find you,' the child said, in excellent English for her age. Her big round eyes observed Mila's wet hair, the beach towel sticking out of her bag. 'Have you been snorkelling?'

'I was scuba diving…with Dr Becker.'

Sebastian appeared with the smoothies. His tall frame threw the young girl into shadow.

'Well, if it isn't our brave canine-fighting superhero. I see you found us.'

'Hello, Dr Becker!' Francoise beamed from beneath her red sun hat. 'My *maman* saw you here. We go home today—back to Bordeaux.'

'Your wounds look much better already, Miss Marchand,' he told her, crouching down to her level to inspect Mila's handiwork on her jaw. 'You'll only have a small scar there, if anyone can even see it at all.'

'I'll be more like a stripe, for braving your ordeal,' Mila followed up.

'Like *your* stripes.' Francoise placed a finger softly to the scars on Mila's left wrist.

'A bit like mine,' she mused aloud.

She didn't pull away. She didn't mind Sebastian looking either. It wasn't like he hadn't been looking at them ever since they'd met. He had called her beautiful on the dive boat earlier on. The memory caused a stir in her heart, but she certainly wasn't about to relive how she'd got her scars in front of strangers.

She couldn't imagine telling Sebastian about her failure to save Annabel. She wouldn't be able to do it, knowing he had met her twin. She couldn't stand the pity on people's faces when she told them how she'd tried to drag her out, too late, just as the car went up in flames. She'd scarred herself for life, trying and failing to get her out through the windscreen, even though Annabel had already been dead when she'd done it.

Francoise took Mila's hand and dropped a tiny wooden dog onto her palm.

'What's this?' Touched, Mila turned it over in her hand and showed it to Sebastian.

'I wanted to say thank you for helping me. It is to protect you from bad dogs.'

'It's a lucky charm,' Sebastian told her, admiring it in her palm. 'You'll see carvings like this all over Indonesia. This one is exceptionally crafted. That's so nice of you, Francoise.'

'It's beautiful,' Mila agreed. 'Thank you, honey, I'll keep it for ever. It will remind me to be brave in the future, like you were.'

Francesca rocked on her flip-flops, looking shy. 'Is Dr Becker your boyfriend?' she asked Mila innocently.

'No, he's not,' she shot back, trying to laugh.

Sebastian gasped in faux shock to make the kid giggle.

'I think he *should* be your boyfriend,' Francoise volunteered. She gave them both a quick hug, reaching her tiny arms around of them, drawing them together. 'You can help people like me together. You can stop all the bad dogs biting other children. I am going to tell everyone about you.'

Sebastian almost dropped the smoothies as their sides were crushed together. For a little kid, she was strong. They watched her skip her way happily up the dust track with her mother.

'Wow.' Sebastian was laughing, resting on one elbow on the bar, even though the tension was a tangible object between them, even bigger than before. 'Looks like you're gathering fans wherever you go.'

'Says *you*. You were really good with her.'

'So were you. Do you really never think about having a family?'

His question caught her off guard and she reacted evasively. 'Me? I'm pretty sure I'd prefer a dog.'

His eyebrows shot up. 'A dog? In that case, maybe you can have Bruno.'

'Bruno needs a permanent home. I'm not here for ever.'

'Shame…' he murmured, and his eyes lingered on her lips just long enough to start a slow simmering burn in her for more of his attention as he sipped his smoothie.

His phone rang then, and saved her having to respond to his obvious flirtation. 'It's Ketut. He'll only just have got home, so something must be wrong. One sec?'

He wandered out to the forecourt with his phone. A couple of twenty-somethings in bikinis looked up at him from the pool, admiring his physique as she did way too often.

His posture quickly told her something bad had happened. She hoped it wasn't serious.

Ketut was a local guy, who worked at the dive shop and drove the boat amongst other things, and she knew Sebastian and Ketut had been good friends since Sebastian had first arrived on the island. He talked about him and Ketut's wife Wayan a lot.

When Sebastian hung up, his mood had done a one-eighty.

'Mila, I have to go,' he said apologetically, slipping into the sandy sandals he'd left by the bar.

He tossed his empty cup expertly into the nearby trash can and hooked his backpack over his shoulder.

'Unless you want to come with me?'

CHAPTER SIX

KETUT FLUNG OPEN the door before they'd even made it up the path. Wayan stood with her arms held out to Sebastian, her belly swollen with their baby, in the doorway of their modest bamboo shack. It was surrounded by terracotta pots and jungle plants, and a moss-covered statue of a Balinese goddess stood to one side. It looked as if it doubled as a bird perch.

'Sebastian! Thank you so much for coming.'

Wayan's voice wobbled and Mila's heart ached as she watched him walk straight into her embrace. It was a real hug, tender and heartfelt, the kind you might give to a family member.

The kind he'd given her on the boat when she'd talked about Annabel's anniversary, she thought, feeling her stomach clench. He must trust her to bring her here. This was personal.

'You know Dr Ricci... Mila? I explained to her a little about the situation on the way over here.

Wayan, you should have called me sooner—I would have come.'

Sebastian guided Mila ahead of him across the threshold, kicking off his sandals on the inside mat. She did the same.

'Wayan didn't want to ruin your dive, so she didn't tell me either,' Ketut explained as he closed the door behind them.

The smell of burning scented candles hit Mila's nostrils as they were ushered into a small, cosy living area. Three dozing cats occupied a tattered pink couch in one corner. Books were stacked haphazardly on chairs, shelves, and even the floor, and soon Ketut was pouring herbal tea from a silver teapot under a whirring fan.

It was simple, but homely. Only the mood was tense.

On the boat on their way over to their house, on a neighbouring island, Sebastian had explained how he spent a lot of time here, so it was almost a second home, and that these two were like his island brother and sister.

Short, fatigued-looking Wayan was likely in her mid-thirties, dressed in a colourful patterned skirt and a white blouse that revealed the lower part of her pregnant belly as she dropped heavily into a tattered armchair. She started biting her nails. On instinct Mila sat beside her just as Sebastian took the wicker chair next to Ketut.

He took the tea cup he was offered. 'So, tell me what's going on, man. What are we dealing with here?'

'I'm hoping you can tell *me*.' Ketut handed Mila a cup too, then pushed a set of ultrasound pictures forward on the coffee table. 'Wayan was given these at Blue Ray. She was too upset to call me, so she came back here and told the cats before she told me.'

'They say the baby will need surgery…' Wayan sniffled.

Her quivering lip turned into a sob and Ketut was beside her in a second, both arms around her shoulders. He was trying to be strong for her, but Mila could tell he was heartbroken. Mila reached for Wayan's hand.

Sebastian pulled his glasses from his backpack, put them on and studied the black and white prints intently.

'Cleft lip and cleft palate,' he confirmed out loud, handing her the X-rays with a deep sigh. 'I'm so sorry, guys, they're right. This is going to have to be fixed in surgery. Usually the procedure's done after about three months...'

'We will love him anyway, of course, Sebastian... Mila. You know we would, no matter what. Even if you can't help us.'

Wayan's sad eyes broke Mila's heart. She had seen a thousand women broken over babies deformed, wounded, stillborn or killed. Again, she put herself in a mother's shoes. The thought of anything happening to a child of her own made her go icy cold... She just wouldn't know what to do if it was her. She'd already proved that in the worst way.

'Why wouldn't he help you?' Mila asked now, looking from Wayan to Sebastian.

'We don't have medical insurance.'

Sebastian stood up, knelt in front of her, and put a hand reassuringly on her knee, over her bright skirt. 'I told you before, you guys did the right thing calling me. I can help you.'

'*We* can help you,' Mila added.

He had brought her here for a reason. She could see the future of this baby meant the world to him, just as his nephew Charlie did, back in Chicago. And he knew she had a way of injecting a certain calm into a situation... Unless that situation involved saving her twin sister from a burning car, in which case she froze like a useless snowman.

Sebastian thought she was stronger than she was. He would never know how the flashbacks and her guilt over Annabel's death still consumed her.

'What can you do, Sebastian? Mila? Will our baby be deformed for ever?' Wayan was pale now, in spite of Sebastian's comforting words.

'Not if we can help it,' Sebastian said defiantly, taking his seat again.

He was looking at Mila from across the room, dragging his hands through his hair. Behind him, through the window, she saw the daylight fading into twilight.

'The surgery is relatively simple, though it sounds quite complex when you try to explain it,' Mila said, finding her voice. 'Once your child is born we'll do another assessment, and there might be a few operations over time, but as for scarring...'

'Minimal,' Sebastian finished for her, meeting her eyes.

They were on the same page. One of the cats leapt from the chair and started curling around her legs. It purred softly in the silence until Ketut spoke.

'By the time the baby is born you might be gone. Sebastian says you're not with us on the island for very long.'

All eyes were on her now—even the cat's. Mila's throat felt dry in spite of her tea. 'I don't know what to say about that…honestly,' she admitted, putting a hand down to pet the purring animal. 'I'm here for a while yet. I don't have an exact departure date. I gave in my notice in London, so I'm pretty flexible, I guess.'

Suddenly she didn't want to leave the island— at least not until this baby was mended and declared healthy. But what could she do? She might have agreed to an undetermined date for the MAC personnel department to arrange her flight out, but still, her life wasn't here. This wasn't her family—as much as she wanted to help them.

Sebastian was biting the inside of his cheek hard, as if he didn't know what to say either…

'Jared, hey, what's up?'

Sebastian kicked the refrigerator door shut, balancing the phone on his shoulder as he carried a bowl of oats and a carton of milk to the countertop.

He was on the verge of running late for a consultation, followed by a scar revision on a car crash victim who was currently on his way from the mainland. But he needed to eat first. Surgery on an empty stomach was never a good idea. He needed all the brain capacity he could muster—especially now.

'Sorry, bro,' Jared said. 'I know it's early over there, but I really need your confirmation for Mom's birthday thing. I need numbers. Does the world's most exclusive surgeon have a plus one in mind this year, or will you be flying solo like last year?'

'I don't know yet,' he told his brother, pulling a spoon from the cutlery drawer.

He noticed a frangipani flower in the drawer—a gift from his cleaner. She hid them everywhere. He slipped it into his pocket idly. He would re-gift it, like he always did, to one of the women in Recovery at the MAC.

'Hi, Uncle Bas!' Charlie's voice was loud on the end of the line, as if he'd stolen the phone for a second.

Sebastian grinned. 'Hello, trouble. Why aren't you in bed?'

It was a time difference of thirteen hours between Chicago and Indonesia, so he rarely got to speak to Charlie.

He saw his reflection in the glass of the window. He looked tired. He hadn't slept much, worrying about Ketut and Wayan and the not so distant departure of Mila Ricci. She might have a while left on Gili Indah, but he'd been realising lately that he wasn't much looking forward to island life without her.

'He's been on a school trip today—haven't you, bud?' Jared said, taking the phone back. 'He's pretty fired up still…'

'We saw dinosaurs!' Charlie enthused in the background, and proceeded to roar like a T-Rex. 'Listen, Uncle Bas!'

Sebastian sniggered. 'Sounds like fun.'

'Sounds like they gave him E-numbers. We'll get him to bed eventually.'

Sebastian smiled. 'How is everyone else?'

'Good, good…same, same. Wrapping up the season. Mom thinks it should be the last one— did she tell you? I think she's finally getting tired of the show.'

Sebastian sat at the breakfast bar, watching Bruno chasing a bird around the yard outside. Jared had said this before, at the end of the last season. And the one before that, too. He didn't want to tell him he'd believe it when he saw it. The network always came back with a better offer.

'I fully support any decision to make this season the last one, but you already know that,' he said instead.

'I know... I know.' Jared let out a sigh. He knew better than to start that conversation again. 'So, back to the party,' he diverted—predictably. 'I think Mom would like it if you brought someone. Laura's rented the Opal Marquee at the Langford—the one in the orchid garden? It's a surprise for Mom. We've invited all her friends from the badminton club. Actually...if you can't think of anyone to bring from your string of island vixens I can ask Theresa. Remember her? That cute blonde dentist from Smile Right in Lincoln Park...'

Sebastian spooned the oats into his mouth as his brother went on, naming women he couldn't care less about getting to know.

'Jared, I'm not going to take some woman to

a party if I'm never going to see her again. And I can only stay three days, remember? I have a lot to do here.'

Jared make a clicking sound with his tongue. 'I get it, bro—your life is there. Can't you think of *anyone* to bring, though? You've come on your own for the last three years.'

'You know why that is.' Sebastian felt his jaw start to tick.

'Yes, I *do* know why. You're paranoid that some pap will catch you doing something shady and make your idyllic island life a misery, But I told you—we don't invite the media to family events, Bas. Any new woman of yours is perfectly safe from prying eyes. None of us wants a repeat of what happened with Klara.'

Sebastian scraped the stool back and dropped his bowl and spoon into the sink—heavily.

Jared's voice softened. 'Sorry to bring it up. I just want to see you happy again, man. You work so hard out there on your own. I hope you're finding time for some fun, too?'

'Actually, there is someone,' he said, before he could stop himself.

'Oh, yeah?'

'I'm not sure she can come with me to Chicago, however. Technically, she's only here on a short-term placement.' He grabbed his backpack and sunglasses, locked the door behind him and patted Bruno in the garden on his way out. 'She's new at the MAC,' he said reluctantly, making sure to close the gates properly.

'Wow. OK…'

Jared drew a breath through his teeth and Sebastian could picture the look on his brother's face.

'You know how I feel about mixing business with pleasure, but I guess that's up to you. Why can't you bring her?'

'For a start we're colleagues—even if it's temporary,' he said, lowering his voice as he walked towards the main MAC building. 'And we're friends too… I think. God, we haven't even been on a date, or anything. I just…'

'You just want to get in her pants before she leaves for good?'

'No, Jared.' He rolled his eyes to the blue sky. 'It's more than that. She's…she's different. Anyway, we have too much to do here, so we can't both be getting on a plane…'

'Stop making excuses, Bas. You deserve a vacation, don't you? And you deserve a decent woman at your side. It's been a long time, bro, since you and Klara broke up.'

'I know.'

'Tell me about this woman! Where's she from?'

Encouraged by his brother's rare enthusiasm for anything that didn't involve the show, Sebastian told Jared a few minor details as he walked—but nothing that would enable him to search for her online. He trusted Jared, of course, but he wouldn't put Mila's privacy in jeopardy for anything.

He spotted Tilda Holt, basking in the sun on a lounger by the swimming pool already. She was recovering from her non-invasive face lift with a cheeky Bloody Mary. He hoped it was a virgin Bloody Mary. He returned her cheery wave and then, remembering the flower in his pocket, turned back and presented it to her with a flourish, his phone still pressed to his ear.

For you, he mouthed in silence.

Her new crease-free eyes shone with delight. She thanked him profusely and proudly placed the tiny white and yellow flower in her hair.

Hugo O'Shea waved enthusiastically from his seat at a table on the sand, looking up from his laptop. He was still hanging around after his enlargement procedure—'working remotely in Recovery,' or so he'd said.

Something about him made Sebastian bristle as he chatted on with Jared. He didn't trust the guy.

But Sebastian's mind was half in the moment, in the MAC's grounds with his patients, and half on the penthouse balcony back home, on showing Mila the views of Belmont Harbour and the lakefront. She'd get a kick out of Charlie, too... He could tell she liked kids a lot, even if she maintained she would prefer a dog herself.

'*Ask* her, bro,' Jared demanded, when he told him he really had to run.

Sebastian swung into the air-conditioned reception area. Mila looked up from the desk, where she and Rachel were studying some papers.

'Hey,' they said at the same time.

Mila was wearing lipstick. He didn't notice anything about Rachel.

God he really wanted to be alone with Mila right now. They'd both been so busy he hadn't seen her much in the last week. But tonight they'd be alone for some of the time. Maybe he should ask her to accompany him to Chicago then.

He pushed the thought aside instantly. He should absolutely *not* do that. They were professional colleagues. Besides, Jared might think the media would leave Sebastian alone in Chicago, and Jared might think he was being exceptionally paranoid, but there were plusses to being paranoid. Being paranoid meant he would never mess up again. Being paranoid meant he would never hurt another woman to the point of her refusing ever to speak to him or see him again.

Sebastian had never said it, and he barely acknowledged it even to himself, but what had happened with Klara had affected him deeply. He would never subject another woman—especially Mila, who clearly had her own vulnerable past to protect—to anything like that again.

'Wayan can really cook,' Mila groaned, putting a hand to her full stomach. 'That veggie *rendang* was probably the best thing I've ever eaten. How do you say delicious again?'

'In Indonesian? *Lezat.*' Sebastian smiled.

He held out an arm to help her step back into the tiny boat and Mila felt the butterflies instantly overpowering her satiated stomach. The water was warm and inviting under her feet, swishing up her legs, almost to the hem of her skirt. The stars were out in force.

With their busy schedules it had taken over a week to arrange another trip for her and Sebastian to see Wayan and Ketut at the same time.

Wayan had made them a *lezat* Indonesian feast that defied all logic, coming from her tiny kitchen, and the conversation had flowed easily—from the cleft palate surgery and scar repair to general pregnancy issues and the brand-new project Sebastian was developing in Bali—a retreat for recovering patients on the mainland.

Mila had also heard countless stories of Sebastian and Ketut's island endeavours, and had been charmed by the way he conducted himself around his adopted family. She'd been about to cancel tonight, out of sheer exhaustion and nightmares three nights running—but, while she needed rest, the thought of being around Sebastian again outside of the MAC was like a comfort blanket somehow.

She admired him and she respected him. Which only served to fuel her growing attraction to him.

She sat on the wooden slats of the tiny fishing boat's seat, watching his muscles flex as he pushed it out from the beach and hopped in. The butterflies swooped in again as he sat down and started the motor. His knee in khaki shorts brushed hers so lightly she might not have felt it if she hadn't been so acutely aware of his closeness.

'Beautiful night,' he said, gesturing up to the stars.

She murmured agreement and looked to the sky. She could feel him watching her. Their mutual attraction was undeniable. She'd seen the looks Ketut had given him, too, and the not so secret smiles between Ketut and Wayan at the dinner table. She knew she lit up in his presence, and that whenever that happened her worries drifted off. But all too often they sprang back unannounced.

Annabel had met him first. Annabel was the one he'd liked first. She had no business entertaining this attraction. Twins did not ever go after the same guy, and those rules hadn't changed just because Annabel was dead.

She shifted slightly, so they were no longer touching. If he noticed her futile attempt at creating distance he said nothing. The boat was skimming the ocean, heading back to the island.

'Did you know the oldest map of the night sky is a map of the Orion constellation?' Mila said, to fill the excruciating silence. 'They found it carved on a mammoth tusk.'

'A mammoth tusk? Really?'

'They think it was carved over thirty-two thousand years ago,' she continued.

Sebastian was looking at her in admiration. She liked it when she taught him things he didn't know.

'So, you're interested in the stars, Doctor?'

'The ones in the sky, yes—not so much the ones on television.'

She was teasing him, and she knew he knew it.

Sebastian grinned at the horizon, one hand steering the boat. 'Are you calling me a star, Dr Ricci?'

'Maybe…'

'A fallen star?'

'Maybe.' She smiled in spite of herself. 'You know how to turn your shine on, though, don't you? Tilda Holt showed me the flower you gave her. She said she was going to press it and put it in a frame.'

Sebastian chuckled. The night was calm and still around the chugging boat. The moon was a thumbnail in the sky. Mila pulled her loose hair over one shoulder to hold it. The wind was tugging it in all directions, along with her white knee-length dress.

'Seriously, we used to study the stars…me and Annabel. But not so much as I did on my own, when I was deployed in the Middle East.'

'Really? You had time to stargaze out there?'

'The quiet nights were the scariest sometimes,' she confessed.

She wondered again why she found it so easy to talk to him about some things, and other things felt impossible to address…like what he might or might not have done with Annabel.

'We never knew what was coming next,' she continued, fighting a vision of Annabel as she pictured her suddenly, right there in the boat with them. 'There wasn't much else you could do on those nights but wish on the stars that the worst would never happen. That's Scorpius—see the long, curving tail?'

She pointed to a constellation above them. Sebastian slowed the boat. It made her heart speed up.

'I see it,' he told her, cutting the engine and shifting on the seat. 'And just to the east…that's what the Balinese call Danau—*danau* means lake. If you want to learn more there's an app. You just point your phone up and it tells you—'

'Stop.' She cut him off.

'What?' He looked alarmed. His knee was back against hers.

'There's an app that you can point at the stars and it tells you what they are? *All* these stars? How is that even possible?'

Sebastian laughed out loud again. The sound was so unexpected it shocked her into laughing herself.

'You're amazing—do you know that?' he said, with genuine affection.

Mila's heart kept on thudding. The way he was looking at her… The engine was still off. They were facing each other now on the seat, so close she could see the lights from the surrounding boats reflected in his eyes.

'I'm not kidding about the app,' he informed her. 'Wait till you see the Zodiacal light.'

'What's that?' she croaked, searching his warm eyes for reasons to back off, to stop this thing before it started. She could feel it coming.

'That's a free show from the skies here that you won't want to miss. It hovers like a cloud over those mountains at sunrise or sunset. It's basically sunlight, reflecting off dust grains that are left over from whatever created our solar system over four and a half billion years ago. They just go round and round, circling the sun in the inner solar system. All these grains...'

Her heart was beating wildly now. The air felt thick and hot, and the back of her neck was damp.

'Sounds like a lot of grains.'

He shifted even closer to her. 'A *whole* lot of grains.'

Sebastian reached a hand to her face and cupped her chin, stroked a thumb softly across her lips. It felt as if time stood still. Her mind went blank.

'You know something?' he said after a pause. His eyes seemed to be clouded over with longing. 'It's not just the fact that I shouldn't have you that makes me want you.'

Mila swallowed. All the hairs on her body stood to attention as he trailed his thumb across her cheek. He made a sound like a strangled groan that spoke straight to her churning insides.

'I know this could be complicated, but...do you

even know how hard it is, Mila, keeping away from you…?'

His fingers made tangles in her hair, drawing her face even closer to his with each knot.

'Tell me to stay away and I will,' he whispered, but his lips were so close, and his fingers weren't leaving her hair.

'Don't stay away.'

It was Mila who caved in first and kissed him.

Sebastian's tongue was like his hands—soft at first, then harder, more possessive. His slight stubble razored her chin as her own hands found his hair, felt the delicious softness of it in her fingers. He was urging her closer, as close as they could get on the seat of the bobbing boat. He drew her legs around him, his kisses firing up parts of her that had been dormant way too long.

Mila was so caught up in the thrill of this new connection that she almost forgot who or where she was. So the sound of the swinging boom from an approaching boat and several panicked cries came completely as a surprise.

CHAPTER SEVEN

THE MAN IN the yellow shirt didn't see his boat's boom lunging violently towards him, but Sebastian heard the crack as it hit him in the face and chest.

'Oh, my God...' Mila fists dropped from his hair to the sides of the rocking boat as they were forced apart in a flash. 'What's happened?'

There was blood on the deck of the other boat already. Sebastian saw it glimmering in the floodlights as he re-started the engine and inched closer, standing to see over the side. It was a sailing catamaran, three times the size of theirs, but there looked to be hardly anyone on it.

Mila's knuckles were as white as her dress as she gripped the boat's edge. 'I can't see anyone injured...'

'He's on the floor.'

Sebastian steered the boat as close as he could get. A woman in a long pink dress was shrieking uncontrollably, hunched over the motionless body of her friend, or maybe he was her lover. Three more men and a woman were doing their best to swing the boom back into place and secure it.

'Don't move him!' Mila shouted from their boat.

He watched as she lifted the boat seat and grabbed two medical kits. He made sure all of the MAC's boats had them on board, and he always brought his own.

Unsurprisingly to Sebastian, Mila needed no help climbing over the side of the boat, and in less than three seconds flat she was barefoot on the catamaran, crouched at the man's side.

'Help me, please—he's out cold!' The woman in the pink dress was beside herself.

Sebastian threw a rope onto the other boat's deck, jumped across himself and hurriedly tied the boats together, impressed by Mila's quick action. The medical bag was already open and she was supporting their victim's head on her own lap, instructing someone to get a cushion.

'What's his name?' Mila checked the man's pupils and pulse.

'John—he's John Griffiths, my husband. I'm

Janet. Something must have got loose on the boom. Oh, my God...the blood.'

'Get me some clean towels,' Mila ordered the others on deck.

She had sprung into doctor mode so fast it was almost as if the woman Sebastian had just kissed so passionately was another person entirely.

'Where did this glass come from?' she asked next, indicating the broken shards all around them on the hardwood decking.

He had only just noticed them himself.

'We were drinking champagne,' the woman explained, raking a hand through her thick bleached blonde hair. She looked guiltily to Sebastian. Then she lowered her head over her husband, weeping and clutching his lifeless hand.

Sebastian tried not to pass judgement as he prepared for evacuation. They were fairly close to shore. The island's nightlife was still pumping on the tourist side—he could smell the beachfront barbecue dinners from here. Maybe they'd been sailing drunk...maybe they hadn't. But it wouldn't be the first time someone had come to a 'party island' and got a little too complacent about the way the ocean worked.

He pulled out his phone and dialled the Blue Ray, telling Agung where they were.

'Agung's sending help to the harbour—let's get him back quickly,' he told Mila, hurrying to her side.

Mila was strapping an oxygen mask to their patient's head, being careful not to move him any more than was necessary. He was still out cold.

The water was deep out here, rocking the boat as if it was nothing but a fragile toy. With both engines off it was enough to make anyone feel seasick. Maybe that was why Mila looked so ghostly pale.

'Tell him we have a suspected pulmonary contusion, broken nose, and I'm pretty sure a shattered left eye socket,' she said.

He relayed the message, then hung up. He fought the urge to ask if she was OK. Of course she was OK. She was being her usual professional self. But he knew she probably hadn't been involved in an emergency at sea before—she'd been stationed in the desert, after all.

Sebastian had seen a couple of deaths at sea caused by booms. If they didn't sweep people overboard, their lines were trip hazards. In this case he could already agree with Mila. The boom's swinging power had broken this man's nose…at least.

Mila's heart didn't stop its mad pounding the whole time they were transporting their patient to shore.

John's wife, Janet, continued to grip her arm as John was loaded onto a stretcher bound for the clinic. She was seemingly in shock and unable to speak. The petite blonde in her mid-forties wore more dramatic jewellery than Mila had ever seen: bangles, beaded necklaces, earrings shaped like mermaids holding coconuts.

And her wedding ring was just as flashy, Mila noted—a huge sparkling jewel on a silver band. She focused on that as she took her hand in re-assurance.

In spite of her being aware of her bare feet sinking into the wet sand, and all the stars and flashlights and equipment beeping around John, Mila felt only half there. First the kiss. Then all that blood on the deck. The swerving of the boat…the way it had all happened so suddenly. Despite her training, it had totally thrown her.

* * *

'X-rays show his nose is broken,' Agung confirmed ruefully, soon after they'd arrived at Blue Ray and were all standing in the critical care unit, observing the monitor. Mr Griffiths was on breathing support, but the monitor kept blinking on and off. It was only when Sebastian slammed a hand to the side that the screen stayed lit.

'Damn thing... Don't worry—the new one's been ordered.'

'He's also fractured several bones in his left eye socket,' Agung said. 'Good spot, Dr Ricci.'

Mila caught Sebastian's look of admiration and approval. No doubt they were all impressed with her keen eye, but she wasn't here for compliments. She'd seen worse—much worse. She was trained to see the detail in the fall-out.

If anything, she was embarrassed and annoyed that Sebastian had spotted her ashen face and the way she'd stalled back there, after seeing all that blood. He hadn't asked if she was OK in front of those people, but he'd been about to—she'd seen it in his eyes.

Maybe they should have tried to call out a warning. Maybe this could have been prevented if they hadn't been so lost in kissing each other like that.

She dug her fingernails fiercely into her palms, internalising her self-loathing. Janet Griffiths was looking to her to be strong, and John would need her soon.

'I'm scheduling him for surgery right after the physician's done with the realignment.' Sebastian cut into her thoughts. 'Emergency reconstruction. We'll get him over to the MAC when he's stable. I'll go now.'

'What can I do?' she asked.

Sebastian ushered her into the corner behind the door. His brown eyes were flecked with concern. 'Stay with Mrs Griffiths till her daughter arrives, if you don't mind. Or Nurse Viv starts her shift soon...'

'Yes, of course. I'll stay here till then.'

A volunteer was helping the distraught Janet Griffiths, now wearing a borrowed jacket, over to a seat in the waiting area.

Sebastian lowered his voice, leaning in to Mila. His breath on her ear made her want to reach for him, but she crossed her arms over her chest instead.

'Mila, I'm so sorry.'

'Don't say it, Sebastian.'

He urged her further behind the door, so no one would see or hear. 'Did that freak you out back there?'

'Sebastian, I kissed you too…'

'I meant the boat, the accident—not our kiss…'

'This is my job. I'm used to it.'

His brow furrowed. 'You turned completely white, Mila.'

She looked at her feet, still sandy in her shoes. Guilt raged through her like a fire. It was Annabel's accident all over again. She hadn't been paying attention to her surroundings and she'd been caught totally off-guard. She'd promised herself that would never happen again, and it just had. She'd also promised herself that she wouldn't let her attraction to Sebastian get the better of her.

'It's not me you should be worried about,' she managed.

'John Griffiths will be fine, Mila. You probably saved his life.'

She folded her arms tighter, building a wall, but she knew it was too late for that. She'd kissed him first. The resulting guilt and tension were unbearable, but she wasn't having this conversation here.

'We'll talk later,' Sebastian told her, as Agung called him away.

And it took every ounce of her strength to resume normality for poor Janet Griffiths.

CHAPTER EIGHT

IT WAS FIVE days since their kiss. Sebastian had been trying to get her alone outside of the MAC for dinner, a drink, a dive...but Mila had apparently been trying even harder to ensure they were surrounded by people at all times. She was avoiding him—he knew it. He had crossed a line with that kiss—they both had—and Mila probably felt that being intimate with him...her employer...had been some kind of immoral move.

Or was it something else?

He couldn't think why else she would be acting this way. Maybe it *was* less than ideal to be making out with his employee on a fishing boat after dining with his friends, but so what? He couldn't get her out of his mind.

Today, though, she couldn't avoid him.

'Morning,' he said, as she approached him on the outside terrace of the MAC.

'Morning, Dr Becker.'

She looked around her, pulling her sunglasses down over her eyes. Several patients were looking their way from the breakfast tables and pretending not to. One of them was Hugo O'Shea.

'Ready to set sail to the mainland?' he asked, starting down the steps.

She followed him, light on her feet in brown sandals and a blue striped dress. 'This won't take all day, will it?'

'Not all day, no. I do believe the staff have transported John and Janet Griffiths to the harbour already, with their luggage. They'll meet us at the boat.'

Sebastian had been in the reception area last night when Mila had promised Mrs Griffiths that she would accompany the couple back to the mainland. It was time for them to leave the island, after their ill-fated vacation, and fly home from Bali, but the couple were understandably a little apprehensive about making the crossing after what had happened on the catamaran. Mila had offered to go with them, for company.

He knew Mila probably wanted some time off the island without him. But he'd offered to go with them. In fact he'd told them, he'd do better than that. He would take them all on the MAC's private boat. He had two new monitors to collect from Bali, anyway, along with a few other chores to get done.

Mila had gone quiet when he'd offered, as if she was annoyed. But *he* was annoyed by her refusal to be alone with him—that was what Klara had done before she'd left him. She'd just flat-out refused to talk. Nothing put him more on edge than when people refused to discuss their problems like adults.

It wasn't all his fault, though, this thing with Mila. He'd told her on the boat that he would stay away from her if she wanted him to, but she had kissed him first. Whatever might have changed between them since then, they definitely needed to talk about it.

'Can I ask you a quick question, Dr Becker?'

Hugo O'Shea appeared in front of them suddenly, blocking their exit at the gates. His hair and beard were dyed bright blue again, bluer than ever before. Where on earth had he got that hair dye on an island this size? Sebastian thought, half amused. He must have brought it with him.

'Is everything OK?' Sebastian asked, trying to inch around him.

'You mean with this?' Hugo gestured to his

newly enhanced groin area and grinned. 'Couldn't be better, This is about something else. I have a commission, Dr Becker, to write an exclusive story on you and your work here on the island. What drove you from Chicago? What brought you here?' His eyes fell on Mila. 'What keeps you here?'

Mila crossed her arms. Sebastian couldn't read her eyes behind her sunglasses, but her body language suggested she would rather be anywhere than here, with them.

'I have the agreement right here for you to read and sign.' Hugo pulled a piece of paper from the pocket of his shorts and thrust it at Sebastian. 'It's time we got moving. It's great publicity for the MAC. We can do the interview wherever you like. On a boat at sunset, maybe—it doesn't matter. This is your side of the story for *USA World*. It's a big magazine, Dr Becker…think about it. Your chance to explain all about Klara, your ex…'

'I know who Klara is, thank you,' he snapped. 'And my answer is no.' Sebastian folded the paper in one hand against his thigh, then squeezed his fist around it, scrunching it up. 'Now, if you'll excuse us, we have to go.'

'Are you sure you won't just—?'

'No. And I'd like to remind you about the NDA you signed before coming here, Mr O'Shea.'

He gave Hugo the mangled piece of paper, ignoring his look of shock and horror, then put a hand to Mila's back and walked them quickly up the path, to where a horse and cart were waiting to take them to the harbour.

Bali was crazy, loud, and a shock to her senses after weeks on the much quieter Gili Indah. Mila wasn't used to seeing cars or motorbikes any more. Hordes of tourists were crowding the jetty or sitting with their bags on the beach, drinking beers, waiting for their transfers. Catamarans and boats bobbed everywhere, but Sebastian's yacht was catching the most attention.

Bright white and gleaming, with three bedrooms and an indoor lounge bigger than her last apartment, it was clearly the prize of a very rich man. She hadn't said so on the journey over here—she'd chatted to Janet most of the way, and besides he'd seemed distant, probably because of Hugo O'Shea—but she'd felt like a VIP the whole time, reclining in a leather couch while the ocean sped by through the windows.

Everything Sebastian surrounded himself with

on the island was modest, and gave no hint of the billionaire lifestyle he probably enjoyed everywhere else. This was like seeing a new side of him—a taster of his old life, maybe. She couldn't help wonder what his place in Chicago was like.

'Do you think we'll make it to the hospital before the rain starts?' Janet asked now, casting her eyes to the heavy, grey sky.

Mila had only just noticed the change. The port was heaving and John was being wheeled towards the waiting ambulance, Sebastian and a paramedic at his side.

'You'll be fine,' Mila told her. 'You're in good hands, and John is making a great recovery. The hospital will arrange for your hotel and airport transfers once they've given him the final go-ahead to fly tomorrow.'

'I can't thank you enough for everything you've done.' Janet took her hands in hers and her bangles jingled on her arms as she squeezed them. 'I know I've said this a hundred times, Dr Ricci. But we might have lost him if it wasn't for you.'

Mila extended a warm smile. 'Well, I'm happy we were there,' she replied.

What else could she say? She was more than happy to have been able to help John Griffiths, of course, in spite of the resulting situation she had put herself in with Sebastian.

Her dreams had changed since then. Annabel was in them all—sometimes alive and dancing, sometimes exactly as she had been when Mila had found her in the car—and sometimes it was herself in the car, Annabel and Sebastian were trying to get *her* out.

It had sent her spiralling into a world of confusion. She'd been hoping for a day to herself over here, to hire a driver and see some of Bali, do some much-needed thinking, but Sebastian had encroached on her plans by coming, too.

'So, forgive me…but I can't not ask you before we go. You and Dr Becker *are* an item, am I right?'

Janet's green eyes flooded with mischief suddenly and Mila realised she'd been gazing absently in Sebastian's direction. He was talking on his phone now, an umbrella tucked under one arm.

She shifted her bag awkwardly onto the other shoulder. 'Not exactly.'

Janet obviously didn't believe her. What the hell?, Mila thought. They were leaving anyway.

She scrunched up her nose. 'There is…something there,' she admitted. 'But it's complicated. And I'm not here for long.'

'Then you'd better get a move on! I met my John at work, by the way. He was a new, arrogant theatre director—I was a new, pushy production manager. We argued like crazy—Shakespearean proportions—till we realised it was actually love and not hate we felt for each other. He proposed on the stage in front of our audience. Over a thousand people saw me cry.'

She held up her big sparkly ring and Mila felt a rush of longing—not for the ring, but for the deep, mutual love Janet had found. It was the kind of love Sebastian had once felt for Klara, she thought, surprising herself with her envy of a woman she had never met.

Janet put a hand to her arm. 'I saw you two out on that dive boat, before the accident. And I've seen the way he looks at you.' Her seashell earrings swung like pendulums and jingled along with her bangles as she leaned in to speak in her ear. 'Everyone adored him on that show— his brother Jared, too. Quite the handsome partnership. They wrote some terrible things about him when he left…something about his ex-girl-friend…'

'I never watched it.'

Janet looked shocked. 'OK. Well, it was years ago, anyway,' she said flippantly. 'And who knows? Maybe all that had to happen just so he could find his way to *you*.' She flattened a hand to her heart dramatically, then shook her head, smiling. 'Sorry…ever the romantic, me!'

Sebastian was heading towards them through the crowds, head down, baseball hat on, still talking on his phone. A couple of people were trying to take photos without him knowing. Women in particular were staring at him.

Mila realised she had probably underestimated the impact his presence on the show had made, despite him leaving more than three years ago, and how popular it had really been and still was. No one paid him this much attention on the island.

'You're all set Mrs Griffiths.' Sebastian slid the phone into his top pocket, then adjusted his hat on his head. 'We're going to leave you in the ambulance crew's capable hands. Dr Ricci and I have an appointment.'

'Limitations live only in our minds—don't forget that,' Janet quoted conspiratorially in her ear, before she gave Mila a huge hug and left.

Instantly the busy harbour seemed to close in. It was just Mila and Sebastian and the thunder starting to rumble on the horizon.

'Are you ready?'

Mila was still distracted by Janet's words. 'What for? Isn't someone delivering a patient monitor for us to take back later?'

'The plan just changed—that was them on the phone. They can't deliver it for a couple more hours. Bali traffic—you know the deal. There's something I need to do. If you decide to come with me it'll give you a chance to see some of Bali with a driver I trust.' He paused. 'Unless you'd prefer to go your own way and meet up later? It's up to you.'

She deserved the disparaging tone in his voice—she knew she did. She also knew they probably needed to talk about what had happened. And Annabel. She couldn't avoid discussing *that* with him any longer.

Sebastian was inching towards the road, where a shiny chauffeur-driven car with blacked-out windows was pulling up in the dust. He looked as though he was exiting the scene whether she went with him or not.

CHAPTER NINE

SEBASTIAN PULLED ON the crisp white shirt, sleeve by sleeve, and buttoned it up in front of the mirror. He studied his jawline in the light, frowning at his reflection. He should have shaved, but it would have to do. He could use a haircut, too.

'How do I look?' he asked, sweeping the curtain aside dramatically and squaring his shoulders in the tailor-made suit. 'Do you think anyone would guess I spend half my life in scrubs and the other half in a wetsuit?'

Mila stood up from the plush white seat. She put the book of designs down on the table, next to a dish of frangipanis. Her eyes appraised the navy blue pinstripe jacket and he realised, feeling some small element of doubt over his own sanity, that even though he knew he looked good he was still seeking her approval.

She trailed her gaze up his body, from shoes to shirt collar, not giving anything away. 'What's the occasion?' she asked.

'My mother's seventieth birthday party. I have to go back to Chicago.'

He hadn't asked her to accompany him, of course. Maybe he would have done if she hadn't spent most of the last week trying to avoid him.

She raised her eyebrows. 'I recall you mentioning something about that. When is that? Before or after I leave the island?'

'I don't think we've talked about your exact leaving dates yet, have we?' he said evasively.

Mila seemed closed off—distracted, even—so now was clearly not the time to discuss it. She was glancing at the rain outside, and the palms lashing at the tailor's windows. There was a storm on the way, all right. It was only supposed to be a quick downpour, but...

'This is definitely getting worse,' she announced, right as his cell phone buzzed again.

It was the delivery guy, delaying the monitor's arrival yet again.

'They might not get it to us till the morning now,' he told her with a frown.

Mila looked like a deer who wanted nothing more than to run away from his headlights. 'What will we do till then?'

'You stay here. I make something for you,' the

tailor cut in. 'Something beautiful. I think blue is your colour!'

Mila turned, holding up her hand. 'Oh, no, that's OK. I don't have anything to...'

'It not take long.'

Sebastian watched Mila in the mirror as Anya, his favourite tailor, bustled off to the storeroom. She came back three seconds later with armfuls of fabric. Before Mila could dissuade her, the tailor was pulling out a tape measure, holding her arms out one by one, whirring around her in her patterned sarong. Then Anya got to her knees and measured each leg, then her hips, waist and bust—quickly, efficiently, enthusiastically.

'You look at designs. I get you samples!'

'Get something made. We can have someone bring it over to the island later,' he told Mila.

He'd been coming here for years, but he'd never brought a woman with him. No wonder they were treating her like royalty.

She shook her head though, resolute. 'No, really... I don't need anything, Sebastian.'

He cocked an eyebrow at her, pulling the shirt off and reaching for another one. This was pale pink. He pulled it on with the curtain still open. He wasn't afraid to wear pink.

He caught Mila in the mirror, biting her lip, watching him dress. 'Have I met the one woman in the world who *doesn't* want a dress made for her?'

'I've never had a dress made for me before, if I'm honest.'

The tailor seemed to notice the way she was covering her arms. 'This one?' She jabbed a finger to a long-sleeved floaty dress in the design book.

Mila let out a defeated sigh. 'OK, fine…yes. I like the ones with long sleeves, actually.'

'Please make whatever dress she wants, Anya. She will find an occasion to wear it.'

Mila looked perplexed. 'Why are you being so nice to me after…?'

'I have no idea,' he grunted. 'Maybe because you're driving me crazy.'

He swiped the curtain closed before she could respond. Anya shuffled quietly into the back room, and he heard Mila stepping closer to his curtain.

She exhaled deeply. 'Look, Sebastian, I'm sorry, OK?'

His irritation faded when he heard the anguish in her voice.

'I'm sorry I've been shutting you out after what happened. You have every right to be annoyed with me. And I know it must be driving you crazy, because you did nothing wrong. I kissed *you* first. It's just…we have to work together, so…'

He stayed quiet. He sat down on the stool in the changing room, put his head in his hands for a moment. This was what he'd wanted to hear— kind of. But he still needed answers she hadn't yet supplied him with.

He couldn't talk with her here. The tailor was tottering in again already.

'I think we should go my place—it's not so far from here,' he said eventually. 'We can ride this storm out there.' He started unbuttoning the pink shirt and pulling off the dress trousers. 'It's not safe on the yacht right now.'

'You have a place close by?' Mila was standing just behind the curtain. Her silhouette looked stock-still through the fabric.

'He has many house,' the store manager whispered. 'Dr Becker very rich. You very lucky lady. You want dress? I send to island when ready.'

'Yes, she wants the dress—thank you, Anya.

And please keep her measurements on file.' He stepped from the changing room, holding his new garments. 'Who knows? We might be needing you again.' He took out his wallet.

'What are you doing? Sebastian, really, I don't need...'

'Just let me do this for you, Mila. You deserve it. We'll take all these, please, Anya—excellent fit as usual. You really do have skills like no other.'

He went about paying for everything and then, holding the store door open for Mila, reached for the umbrella he'd left in the corner and led them back outside into the storm.

'Which is your place?'

Mila was flummoxed. The rain was coming down in thick, hard slashes, turning the hem of her blue-striped dress an even darker blue and whipping up the ocean of palm trees around them. They had hardly seen anything of Bali, even though he'd promised—not that it was Sebastian's fault. The rain had concealed everything through the car windows.

'We need to take the funicular railway up to the top.'

He held the umbrella over her, to protect her as far as possible from the ever-imposing rain, and snaked an arm around her waist so they could both take shelter. The gesture had her tensing slightly, even though she liked it.

'Of *course* you would have the villa on top of the mountain,' she said out loud.

He smiled, walking them towards the small red carriage on a track. It looked like the start of a rollercoaster, and promised a rickety journey up through the steep green terrain. They were right at the bottom level of some kind of terraced valley. Each level seemed to house a different villa.

'Is it safe?' Mila had travelled in scarier conditions in her time, but she wasn't too thrilled about taking a wobbly funicular in a storm.

'It's perfectly safe. I would never take you anywhere that wasn't safe.'

Sebastian tightened his arm around her protectively and at the waiting carriage flipped the latch, urging her inside ahead of him. Leaves thrashed the Perspex windows, jostling them along with the wind as he slammed the door behind them and dropped to the seat beside her.

He pushed a hand through his wet hair. Droplets landed on her arm.

'Maybe someone called the witch doctor,' he said.

'Witch doctor?'

'Practitioners of the dark arts, if you believe in that kind of thing. They're called *dukuns* in Indonesia, and they can control the weather. Amongst other things.'

Mila felt far away from everything and everyone as Sebastian pressed a big red button and the carriage shuddered into motion. They'd already headed past smoky mountains, mystic grey temples covered in carvings, and endless green pastures to get here. He'd told her all about it, even though she hadn't really been able to see any of it though the rain.

They weren't far from the yacht, but now, with the jungle all around them, it felt remote and exclusive.

They were sitting so close on the tiny seat she could make out each of the thick black hairs along his jawline, dotted with grey. She liked it when he didn't shave for a while.

'People hire the *dukuns* to make it rain. And to stop it raining,' he said.

His shoulder brushed hers near the strap of her dress, giving her goosebumps.

'But I hope they don't make it stop just yet,' he went on. 'I think we need to talk about what happened, don't you?'

'I know,' she relented.

His left arm was stretched across the back of the seat behind her. He smelled like a mixture of surgery, incense, musky soap and rain.

A gust of wind rocked the carriage and her hand found his knee. Behind his head the lush green valley stretched for miles under a blackened sky. The thought of the carriage tumbling down into the valley with both of them in it at the whim of a Balinese witch doctor flashed briefly through her mind.

Annabel was there too, suddenly, in the carriage with them—just like she'd been on the boat before Mila had given in to their overwhelming chemistry and kissed him. It felt too small.

'I bet Hugo O'Shea would love a photo of us right now, in here together,' she tested, trying to fill the silence.

Sebastian shook his head, releasing her fingers. A bolt of lightning lit the sky, followed by more thunder. 'Can you believe that guy?' he asked.

'Why is he still on the island?'

'He says he's been working remotely while he recovers, but now I know he really wants a damn story. He's just been hanging about, waiting for the right time to ask.'

'Why don't you just talk to him? Tell him what you want him to print? You can have the final say over it, surely?'

'I don't talk to the media,' he said bluntly. 'Neither should you.'

'I'm not Klara,' she reminded him, before she could think about it. Janet had clearly got to her, talking about Sebastian's ex.

The carriage had stopped on the top level. Sebastian was quiet.

'Sorry,' she said. 'I know you despise the media because of what happened to Klara. But publicity is not *all* bad, is it? You're doing good things for the island, and people should know about it.'

'Maybe it's none of their business.'

He flung open the door and stepped purposefully from the carriage, opening the umbrella over her as she followed. The subject was clearly closed.

Through the rain she made out the villa. It was smaller than she'd pictured, but undeniably exclusive. A Balinese statue of a lion guarded the carved wooden door. An infinity pool appeared to melt into the jungle all around them.

She was just about to say she'd bet it was beautiful in the sunshine when a dog started to bark uncontrollably. She jumped and her bag fell into a puddle with a thud. The important envelope she'd put in it just that morning drifted straight into the swimming pool...

CHAPTER TEN

'No, no, no!' Mila leaned over and fished the envelope out. She looked visibly upset.

'Stay still.'

Sebastian stepped in front of her, making his body a shield between Mila and the growling black dog. It was nothing like Bruno, his docile rescue animal. He suspected it was more like the one who had bitten poor little Francoise. It was flattened to the floor on its belly now, baring its teeth just inches from the poolside.

Mila started shaking the water off the envelope in distress.

'Get on the porch!' he ordered as the dog started snarling again, louder than before.

Mila froze.

'We won't hurt you,' he soothed, holding his hand up to the dog and risking getting closer for a better look.

It was a bitch. She had scruffy pointed ears,

thick, coarse fur in tortoiseshell swirls, and what looked like a cut on one paw.

He kept his voice low and his movements slight, crouching down in the rain under the umbrella to retrieve Mila's fallen handbag. 'I know you're just scared.'

He threw the bag towards Mil on the porch. The dog kept on snarling but didn't move.

'She might have been hit by a car on the road at the top and got lost trying to get down. She might have been attacked by another dog. We should take her inside,' he said.

Mila had pulled something from her bag. She was holding it in the palm of her hand, clenching and unclenching her fist over it.

He tossed her the key. 'Open the door. There'll be treats on the table—bring me something to give her.'

He watched her shake off her shoes, slide the glass door open and enter the apartment barefoot as he braved putting his fingers closer to the dog's nose.

'We won't hurt you,' he said softly.

Mila reappeared with some of the tiny ginger biscuits the housekeeper always left him. 'These?'

'Those will do.'

He unwrapped one quickly and held it out on his palm. The dog sniffed his hand tentatively before taking the biscuit. Her temperament softened instantly. She seemed to have decided to trust them, thankfully.

'Are you hungry, girl? No collar...no obvious owner.'

Sebastian shook his head. It broke his heart that so many animals were abandoned and ignored. He gave her another treat and was rewarded with a lick from her wet pink tongue.

'We should get you cleaned up. Want to come in with me?'

'Is she OK?' Mila flattened her back to the wall, holding the wet envelope to her chest as he carried the dog past her on the way to the bathroom.

'It's not as bad as I thought—just a flesh wound, I think.'

The white marble floor would be good enough for now. He pulled towels from the top drawer of the wicker bathroom storage unit and the first aid kit from the bottom one.

'Help me lay these down. We can clean up the

cut, give her a couple of stitches. If it's not looking better by morning we'll take her to a vet.'

Her threw her some towels and she crouched beside him. 'Morning? We'll be here till morning, now?'

'We definitely can't take the yacht back in this weather.'

'I know, but...'

'If you want to stay in another villa I'll give you the keys.'

'That's not what I meant...' She paused. 'How many of the villas do you *own*?'

'All of them. But this is the only one that's furnished beyond the basics right now.'

Mila looked stunned.

'What is that you've got there?' He gestured to the other object she was holding in her hand.

She unclenched her palm reluctantly and he felt his eyebrows shoot to his damp hairline.

'You carried that in your bag this whole time?' It was the wooden dog charm that Francoise had given her at the dive shop.

Mila shrugged. 'She did say it was for protection. It didn't help my bag, though, did it?'

'Sorry... I guess it still worked a little, though. The dog seems OK now.'

The dog's paw must be sore, and she'd likely been scared outside in the storm, but otherwise she really did seem OK. She wasn't barking or growling any more, and she seemed to be appreciative of their help. The licks were now coming thick and fast.

It took them about twenty minutes to stitch and bandage her paw. Then they showered in different bathrooms and changed their clothes. Luckily they'd brought more, in case they wound up swimming somewhere.

The rain was still hammering the pool when Mila met him in the open-plan kitchen. He could see it through the floor-to-ceiling windows. He pulled out cold soda and glasses.

'This place is beautiful,' she told him in genuine admiration. 'I love the walls.'

'Thank you. I had an Indonesian designer do those.' He pointed to his favourite mandala feature wall, and then the carved timber hanging plaques. 'And that rug happens to be the softest rug on earth. Try it.'

Mila walked onto the plush cream rug in her bare feet and moaned in pleasure. He chuckled under his breath.

Much like his other place, he had filled the

place with trinkets to make it feel more like a home: wooden and bamboo bowls and baskets, brass and gold utensils, textiles in fabulous colours, gorgeous cushions, glass pineapples…

'What will you do with the other villas?' she asked. 'I'm guessing this is the place you talked about over dinner that night with Wayan and Ketut?'

He nodded, then handed her a glass fizzing with soda. 'I'm hoping Jared will get over here at some point soon. Like I said, this extension of the institute will be more like a health and wellness centre for convalescing trauma patients and people who can't afford the luxury of the MAC. There's a huge building down at the base of the mountain, before you get to the funicular. You wouldn't really have seen it in the rain, I guess. These villas will be the guest quarters. If this really is the last season of the show Jared should have more time, so…'

'They're wrapping up the show for good?'

Mila looked at him in surprise. He hadn't told her this, or anyone for that matter, because he didn't really believe it himself.

'He has said it before and it hasn't happened,'

he explained. 'I guess I'll find out more in person when I go home.'

'You didn't say when you were going back to Chicago?'

'I think it's around the time your official term ends at the MAC,' he replied, evading the question again.

Truthfully, he knew it was exactly the same time as her leaving date. He'd tell her soon, but he couldn't bring himself to think about her leaving yet... Or going to Chicago alone and coming back to find her gone.

He poured some dried fruit snacks into a bowl. The housekeeper always kept provisions here.

Their canine patient barked in the bathroom and Mila flinched. 'Is she OK in there?'

'She's just reminding us she's there. You really don't spend much time around dogs, huh?'

'Not as much as you,' she admitted. 'I don't mind them, but I don't particularly trust them as a species. We found a crazy dog once at a military outpost—bit half of my colleague's face off. We were only trying to help it. Annabel got bitten by a dog once, too. When we were kids in Ibiza.' She paused, then added, 'I felt her pain when happened.'

'Physically?'

Mila followed him to the couch, putting her wet envelope down on the table to dry. 'Yes. On my ankle. It felt like I'd got bitten myself. So strange... Personally I try not to have a thing against dogs. We must treat the insurgents, too, am I right?' She gave a wry smile.

Sebastian couldn't help laughing. 'Insurgents?'

'One time a bomb went off, northeast of our base in Helmand. We found two dead—a British soldier and an Afghan interpreter—and two injured soldiers—a Brit and an Afghan. We treated them both, side by side. If local nationals and insurgents were injured as a result of our conflict they were always entitled to a medevac.'

'That must have been...' He blew a sound out through his lips and shrugged apologetically.

'It was the biggest source of conflict out there for some people. But in my eyes if someone is wounded I have to help them—regardless of who they are. There's no first-come-first-served. If someone's dying and I can help stop that happening I'm going to do it. Wouldn't you?'

He stared at her. What else had she seen out there? 'Yes, I would. Of course.'

'I know you would—actually, you're putting

Ketut and Wayan first, whenever they need you, even if they're not paying customers.' She paused. 'I wish I was going to be here to see the baby.'

'We don't know for certain that you won't be—babies have a habit of coming when they want to, don't forget.'

Mila shifted awkwardly against the frangipani-printed cushions, sipping on her soda. It was strange having her here in this villa. She hadn't even stepped foot inside his place on the island, and he suddenly regretted never asking her there. He'd been concerned someone might see—someone like Hugo O'Shea—but people were always going to talk anyway. And he was always going to be slightly paranoid. It was just the residual effects of his past life in the spotlight.

He wanted to ask if she really had to leave at the end of her term, but he knew people like Mila didn't stick around in one place too long. She had done too much, seen too much of the world, to want to be cooped up on an island for ever...hiding away with him.

'Is that a twin thing?' he ventured now. 'Feeling each other's pain?'

She curled her legs up on the couch. 'It *was* a twin thing—with us, anyway. I always felt it. Whenever she had a headache, I'd always get one, too. It was the strangest thing…that connection. Sometimes when I get headaches now I still think it might be hers I'm feeling, but then I remember it can't be. The pain is all mine.'

'Talk to me about her,' he said, drawing his legs up on the leather couch opposite hers.

'I'll do one better—I'll show you,' she said. 'If it's not ruined.'

'If what isn't ruined?'

Mila reached for the wet envelope, pulling out a photograph that was damp around the edges. She handed it to him.

'You and Annabel,' he stated.

It shouldn't have surprised him, seeing them both together in the photo, but he found himself staring at it, battling a sudden surge of emotion. He couldn't have told them apart, side by side.

'That was the Christmas we got each other the exact same silly scarf without knowing,' she explained.

The twins were grinning in front of an orange sofa in a cosy living room, both wearing a yellow scarf with the words *Crime Scene* knitted into it. Seeing this image now of them both together made her plight and her grief all the more real.

'You brought this with you?' he asked.

'My mother sent me a package from home recently, and this was in it. We shared a bedroom till we were eighteen, and there are still lots of old photos there in boxes. Mum keeps hinting that I should go home and sort it all out with her...throw some things away. I know I have to do it eventually.'

'I can't even imagine how tough that would be...to have to do that for your twin,' he said, as she took the photo back. 'But have you considered that it also might help?'

She stared at the photo, eyes narrowed. 'Maybe. I still see her everywhere. I dream about her all the time.' She paused then, and took a deep breath. 'Sebastian...what happened when Annabel was here? The two of you...what did you do?'

Mila's words took him completely by surprise. Her eyes were closed now, as if she couldn't even face what he might say.

'I need to know, Sebastian. I should have asked you sooner, but I like you, so I couldn't—no, I didn't *want* to hear it. But I really need to know. Did you kiss her, like we...?' She scrunched up her face, as though the very thought caused her physical pain. 'Did you sleep together?'

'No!'

He put his drink down, took hers away, too. Shuffling up close, he reached a hand to her face. She turned into his palm, exhaling in relief.

'Mila, I thought you already knew that nothing happened with me and Annabel?'

'Nothing at all?'

'No—nothing! Maybe a little mild flirting, but it didn't mean anything to either of us. She was just a typical tourist here—to me anyway. She was drinking and dancing and killing it at karaoke. "Total Eclipse of the Heart" never sounded so adorably terrible as she made it sound. She even missed a snorkelling trip because she couldn't get out of bed one morning. Is that what you wanted to know? Mila, she was just like you—but actually nothing like you at all.'

Mila swiped at her eyes, let out a laugh. 'That sounds like Annabel.'

He put his forehead to hers, both hands to her face. His mind was reeling now. Was this why she'd been distant ever since they'd kissed? Not because she was afraid of putting their working relationship in jeopardy, but because she thought he'd already been intimate with her sister?

'God, Mila, I wish you hadn't carried all this around inside you. You should have talked to me sooner.'

Mila reached for him at the same time as he gathered her into his arms. Their mouths collided, and then all he could do was kiss her till they were stumbling their way together to the bedroom.

Mila let him worship her body and revelled in worshipping his. How could she *not* want to be with this man when he treated her as if she was the only woman he'd ever wanted? It was easy to forget everything, even the horrors she'd seen that kept her up most nights, when they were buried in each other.

They found their way together so easily, so perfectly, time after time on the soft satin sheets of his carved wooden bed—and, when sleep finally came for her, for the first time in a long time Mila had no dreams about Annabel, or the accident, or Afghanistan. None at all.

CHAPTER ELEVEN

THE WOMAN HAVING the mastopexy had a small tattoo of a star on her left shoulder. It seemed to shine under the OR lights as Mila guided her to the wall, where she put her into position on her feet.

'We need you standing up for the markings,' she said. 'I hope you're not feeling too nervous, Mrs Pilkington-Blythe?'

Their patient, a well-to-do forty-four-year-old interior decorator and perfume designer from the UK, didn't look as if she was nervous at all. In fact she looked excited.

'Thank you, Dr Ricci, but it's not exactly a nerve-racking thing to get your boobs out once you've had kids, is it?'

Mila took the marker from Sebastian. 'I suppose not.'

'Mine used to be pert—really up here.' Madison Pilkington-Blythe heaved her breasts upwards for a moment towards her chin, creating a cleavage. 'I miss that,' she moaned.

Sebastian's face was the picture of professionalism as he tapped away at the new touchscreen monitor. It was two weeks now since they'd brought two new monitors back on the yacht—one for the MAC and one for the Blue Ray Clinic. They had almost forgotten to pick them up. They had been more than a little preoccupied the morning after the storm...

It still felt like yesterday that they'd spent hours making love in every corner of that bedroom in Bali...right up until the dog had jumped on the bed the next morning, wondering what all the noise was about.

The rain had finally stopped and they'd been late to the harbour. There had probably been a thousand more responsibilities she'd ignored, but something big had changed between them. A new lightness had surrounded her. She'd let this new level of intimacy with a man sweep her away with its depth and passion.

Madison Pilkington-Blythe didn't know any of this, of course. Their patient had just been flown in to the island on a private helicopter. But Mila had made love to Sebastian that very morning in the shower at the dive school, and again back at his house before coming in to do this procedure. Making love to him took her to a different place.

'You'll know what breastfeeding does to your nipples too?' Mrs Pilkington-Blythe was still talking. 'Unless you were one of the lucky ones.'

'I wouldn't know about breastfeeding myself—only from what I see in my patients,' Mila returned absently, starting the marking.

'You don't have children?'

'Not me.'

'I suppose it must be hard meeting someone when you live all the way out here...' Mrs Pilkington-Blythe sounded almost sympathetic. 'But don't you worry, Doctor, you've got time. Don't take too long, though—the later you leave it, the harder it is to get your figure back. Trust me—I know. That's why I'm here.'

'Can I interest you in any particular kind of music?' Sebastian cut in—probably to save her.

On this occasion Mila was grateful. She knew he was listening and the topic put her slightly on edge, because she knew Sebastian wanted kids while she...she couldn't think of anything more terrifying.

'What do you two usually like to listen to?' Mrs Pilkington-Blythe asked.

'We play all kinds of different things in here,' he answered, turning to the old gramophone she knew he'd kept from his father's surgery. 'Dr Ricci has some pretty good moves.' His eyes flicked to hers mischievously and Mila turned her back before her glowing cheeks gave her away.

They worked to the sound of Beethoven, raising their patient's breasts and leaving no hint of the children they'd helped to feed and nourish.

What would it be like, being responsible for someone? A tiny, helpless human? A child who looked a little like her and a little like Sebastian... A child who needed her for food and advice and survival.

It would be...*beautiful*, she thought.

Then Annabel flashed into her head again. Annabel who'd also needed her for survival and who'd died because she hadn't got to her in time.

She had no right even imagining herself with Sebastian's baby, she scolded herself. Not only was she getting too far ahead of herself, but she wasn't fit to be a mother—she hadn't even been able to take care of her sister.

'What's on your mind?' Sebastian asked her, looking at her in mild concern.

'Nothing,' she lied.

'Sebastian? It's me.'

'I know it's you, Jared. I have your number saved in my phone. How's it going?'

He and Mila were on a rare two-hour break from work, and were spending it at his place. He was inside, mixing jasmine tea with ice in a blender, and Mila was outside wearing a red bikini under a see-through sarong. He hadn't anticipated being interrupted.

'I'm calling to find out how you're doing with this photo.'

'Photo? What do you mean?'

Outside, Mila was running the length of the yard with Bruno and the dog they'd rescued on her heels. She'd named her Stormy.

He lowered his voice and crossed to the dish rack for glasses. 'What photo?'

'Social media, bro. Don't you even follow your own hashtags?'

'I try not to.'

'Well, I hate to be the one to break it to you, but some so-called journalist—Hugo O'Shea—

has posted a photo of you and some lady. Interesting caption... And you look pretty damn cosy on board your yacht with this... Mila Ricci. Is she the woman you were telling me about before?'

Sebastian saw red. If he hadn't just given Hugo O'Shea a new penis, he'd be very inclined to chop it off...not that he'd say that out loud.

'Yes, that's her,' he said through gritted teeth. 'How the hell did he get photos of us on the boat? He was at the MAC—he can't have known where we were...'

He trailed off and ran the order of events through his head. Hugo had stopped him on the way to the harbour to ask for that interview. He could have asked around, found out where they were going, when they were due back with the new monitors. He could easily have lined up a photographer.

'I can't believe that guy!'

Jared let out a snort. 'Hey, chill... I was going to say you look cute together. You told me she was "different", and you said you liked her. She doesn't exactly look like she hates *you*, standing behind her with your arms out like you're acting out a scene from *Titanic* either. And is that a…a dog with you in the photos? What were you *doing*?'

Sebastian clenched his jaw. He hadn't exactly been mimicking the *Titanic* movie. When the dog had jumped up behind them on the bow of the yacht he'd been trying to maintain balance on a particularly bumpy wave at the request of their skipper.

He closed his eyes, with his back to the countertop. 'What was the caption?'

'Billionaire Doc Re-enacts Titanic with Mystery Brunette.'

'Great. That's just great.'

Jared was laughing.

Outside Mila was calling to Stormy. She loved that dog already.

'Jared, you know I can't stand this kind of thing. You know what happened before…'

'Listen, forget it—it's just one photo. It doesn't matter. Mila's leaving soon anyway, isn't she?'

Sebastian bit his tongue. 'That's not the point.'

He almost felt Jared's sigh in his ear before his brother said, 'I'm sorry about Klara, bro, you know I am. But this is one photo in over *three* years. No one cares about what happened before. You're doing great work out there. But still you refuse to talk to anyone so the media is feeding off scraps. What do you expect? You're an icon.'

Sebastian's heart was thudding at his ribs. He couldn't process it all.

'Just bring her to the party with you, will you?' Jared said.

Sebastian drummed his fingers angrily against the countertop. He had tried his best to avoid this kind of situation—he'd even put up *'No Photography'* signs around the MAC just in case anyone had ideas. But still… Was nowhere safe?

He could see Klara in his mind's eye, slumped distraught on the kitchen floor after reading that email from the parents of the kids at her school. They'd all turned against her. They'd told her she was unfit to be a teacher—when she'd loved those kids more than anything. And now Mila was about to see first-hand what it was *really* like attempting to date a world-famous surgeon.

'Sebastian? Are you bringing her?'

'I haven't asked her yet,' he snapped. 'How can I ask her *now*? The cameras will be waiting for us at the airport.'

'I think you're being way too paranoid. I went ahead and put you down for a plus-one anyway. Mom's excited to see you. I've sent you tickets for the jet—one's blank, so you can fill in her name if you decide to bring her. I'm looking forward to seeing you too, bro, it's been too long.'

Sebastian was fuming. He stood by the kitchen sink under the air-conditioning, watching Mila and Stormy through the window as Jared changed the topic.

From now on he'd have to be even more careful.

CHAPTER TWELVE

'NEARLY A MILLION likes already,' she said as she turned towards the sink and pulled at the strings of her bikini. 'That's impressive.'

'It's not impressive.'

Sebastian's jaw ticked from left to right as if he was grinding his teeth. He was half scrolling through the comments on his phone, half watching her reflection in the mirror from the bathroom doorway.

The sun was streaming in on her body through the trees overhead. At first Mila had felt self-conscious in this outdoor bathroom at Sebastian's place, but the way he worshipped her body in it had shifted her perspective somewhat.

'Those comments, though...' She was determined to lighten the situation. He had a face like a thunderstorm and they didn't have long before they had to get back to the MAC. 'They're not bad. People are just interested in what you're doing out here.'

'I could do without their interest, Mila. So could you. We shouldn't be seen together.'

She pulled the bikini top off completely, dropped it to the floor beside her. He was behind her in a second, folding his arms around her. Her body seemed to attach itself to his like a magnet, and she was shocked for a second by their reflection in the mirror. He looked for a moment as if he never wanted to let her go. Adrenaline flooded her veins.

'Sebastian. Whatever people think or say about me, I can handle myself,' she told him.

The familiar tingle of anticipation had started in her toes. The more she told herself this was just a temporary fling, that they were entirely incompatible on so many levels, the more she craved being with him.

'I don't doubt that you believe that, soldier,' he rasped in her ear.

She shuddered at his intoxicating closeness. 'I don't need you to protect me.'

'What if I need you to protect *me*?'

He was urging her bikini bottoms down now. She stepped out of them, found the button on his shorts, snapped it open, reached into the shower and flipped the lever.

Warm water gushed onto their heads as he sat her on the seat and lowered himself to his knees between her legs. It was moments like this that Mila lived for lately. She hadn't experienced this level of sexual spontaneity till now. Maybe she had just never let herself really trust anyone this much.

A dog barked.

Sebastian pulled away from her in a second, snatching up a towel. 'What was that?'

He stopped the shower, moved to wrap the towel around her shoulders, but she stood up and grabbed his wrist, taking it from his hands.

'Bruno or Stormy must have seen someone go past the gates, that's all. The gates are locked, so nobody can come in,' she said calmly, and dropped the towel again.

He was so on edge after that social media post. She couldn't appear to be affected; he would just get even more jumpy.

'It was nothing,' she promised.

Sebastian looked as if he wanted to leap over the wall, brandishing a baseball bat, but she urged him back into the shower till he stuck his hands up in surrender, groaning under her mouth and her lips.

She knew the gates were locked. And no one could get over them—he'd told her he'd made sure of that himself a long time ago.

'It's only us,' she assured him. 'No one can see us here. Trust me, Dr Becker... I'm a soldier.'

The girl was out cold. Blood had formed dark splotches on her yellow cotton T-shirt and on the hem of her bleached white shorts.

'Female patient, Zuri Lerato, twelve years old. Looks like she's fallen somehow. She was unconscious when her father found her in the hotel bathroom. There was blood on the floor and walls.'

The glucose machine beeped between Mila and Nurse Viv.

'Forty-three,' Viv reported. 'Blood pressure one-six-seven over ninety-three. Pulse one-twenty-three. O2 sat ninety-two...'

Mila put a hand to the girl's chest. This time she stirred and her eyes fluttered open. She blinked up at the ceiling fan, tried to sit up, but Mila encouraged her back down. 'Don't move,' she told her.

The girl looked as if she was lost for words—as if nothing was familiar and it scared her.

'It's OK, sweetie, you're safe,' Mila soothed, stroking her arm softly. We're all here to help you. Do you remember what happened?'

Zuri just groaned and shook her head. She still looked confused. It was worrying, to say the least. She had clearly fallen, and Mila suspected from the girl's father's account that she had hit her head on the bathroom sink and passed out. She was likely to be in shock, but Mila wanted to get this girl a bedside brain scan.

'Another blood pressure reading, please!'

By now Mila was used to having to be in ten places at once on the island, but today of all days she was finding it almost impossible to keep her mind off Annabel. And as her team took care of a dazed young Zuri she couldn't wait to give herself the all-clear and be alone.

It was the day of the anniversary. She had considered taking the day off, as she'd planned, but things were just too crazy.

Sebastian had a facial scarring consultation over on Bali for a guy who was too fragile to be moved to the island yet. He had stayed in his villa on the mainland last night, and although she'd insisted that she would rather they both continue their duties and stay busy, rather than take time off and dwell on what the day meant for her, she was itching to see him later.

They were going to his favourite diving spot off the island: a night dive just for the two of them.

He'd suggested it himself.

'I know you switch off down there too, like I do. Maybe it will help you finally feel at peace with what happened.'

Mila wasn't sure it would be possible not to think of Annabel constantly on a day like this, but she had agreed to the night dive, grateful for his compassion.

When she was finally able to discharge herself, with Zuri stable in Recovery and Nurse Viv on night watch, she realised just how much tension she had been holding in all day. Walking back to her cosy little villa in the MAC grounds she couldn't wait to be under the water. First, however, she had to call her mother.

She reclined in the hammock on her porch with a cup of hot tea. The moon was rising beyond the palms as she dialled the familiar number.

'How are you, Mum?'

'Oh, my darling, I was hoping you would call. I'm as OK as can be expected.'

'I said I would call. I know today is hard, Mum, and I wish I was there with you.'

Mila closed her eyes to the emotions as tears blurred the trees ahead, feeling the knots start to tighten in her stomach. She'd been doing so well, keeping her cool all day around other people, but her mother's caring voice had the ability to knock the wind from her sails in a heartbeat.

'I'm just about to head out, actually,' her mother informed her.

She swiped at her eyes. 'Where are you going?'

'Just out with a…friend.'

Her mother had paused before the word 'friend' and Mila felt her eyebrows knit together. She stopped swinging the hammock, put her tea on the floor.

'He's taking me to a gallery. There's an exhibition on Tudor England and the reign of King Henry VIII—he knows I'm into that kind of thing.'

'He?' Her mother had never mentioned a male friend—at least not a man who took her to things like art exhibitions. 'Who is "he"?'

'I told you—just a friend. He's good for me, Mila. Today especially.'

Mila decided to store this new information for

another day, when they could talk about it without the shadow of Annabel's death hanging over them.

'I'm glad you have company today, Mum.'

'Have you been keeping busy yourself?' her mother asked. 'With your Dr Becker?'

'He is taking me out soon, yes.'

'Does he know what happened? I mean, does he know what day it is?' Her mother's voice faltered suddenly. 'Oh, my… Sorry, Mila, I thought I had this under control.'

Mila swallowed the urge to cry, too. They'd both done well till now, trying to sound strong for each other, like they usually did.

'He knows today is the day Annabel died,' she told her mother apprehensively. 'But he still doesn't really know exactly what happened.'

'What do you mean, "exactly"?'

'He doesn't know that I failed to help her… help her get out of the car in time.'

'Oh, Mila…'

Her mother's voice was faltering now, and Mila cursed herself. She swung her legs from the hammock and paced the porch, taking in a deep lungful of sea air. She was trying to think of something happy to tell her mother, willing the calm to come back.

'We have been over this before, Mila—so many times. I won't let you blame yourself.'

'I know, but I can't help it, Mum.'

She swallowed back her tears. Sebastian was picking her up soon—she couldn't look as if she'd been crying. He was kind, and understanding, and tolerant of her intermittent bouts of PTSD, but he didn't even know how she'd got the scars on her arms. He probably assumed she'd got them in Afghanistan. Maybe he felt asking her about them might upset her—which was true.

She didn't want him to think any less of her for her failure to save Annabel—especially not now she was falling for him.

It hit her like a brick.

She was absolutely falling for him. It was much more than a brief, casual fling to her now—she'd been missing him badly all day.

'When are you coming home, baby?' her mother asked eventually, just as Mila had known she would.

'Soon, Mum. I haven't forgotten about clearing out our old room...the rest of Annabel's stuff.

It's the first thing we'll do together when I get back, I promise.'

'You're putting it off as much as I am.' Her mother sighed. 'Or maybe you have another reason not to want to come home now?'

Mila couldn't argue with that. 'You know me too well...' she muttered, casting her wet eyes to the clock through the bedroom window.

It was past eight p.m. Sebastian was supposed to have been here twenty minutes ago.

A small, fuzzy torpedo of love hurtled at her the second she was through the gates. Sebastian had given her a spare key, so she could always get in without ringing the buzzer. Usually it felt like breaking the rules, but tonight she didn't care. He wasn't answering his phone and she was starting to get worried.

'Did you miss me, huh? Did you...?'

Stormy and Bruno barked and nuzzled at her ankles as Mila took the steps up to the front porch. She put her homemade paper lantern down on the table by the hammock, careful not to let the dogs damage it in any way.

'That's for Annabel,' she told the nosy animals, ringing the doorbell. 'We're going to set it off on the water from the dive boat, in her memory. You didn't know Annabel, but you would have liked her.'

Stormy cocked her head with her tongue hanging out and Mila patted her affectionately. Sometimes it was nice not to be answered or buried in questions, just acknowledged by a living creature whose sole responsibility was to give and receive unconditional love.

The house was quiet. It seemed to be all locked up.

Frowning to herself, she peeked through the bottom window into the sitting room. The dogs jumped up at the window too, paws to the glass alongside her, probably anticipating a feed.

'Where is he? He was supposed to be back from Bali by now.'

Stormy let out three barks in quick succession. 'I wish I could understand your language.' Mila sighed, then let herself into the house. 'Sebastian!'

Nothing. There were no sounds coming from his bathroom either.

The couch looked so appealing... She was beyond tired and could almost have napped on it. Maybe he was just late coming back. She was more than ready for her night dive. She didn't want to be alone with her thoughts. She didn't want to sleep in case the dreams came back. She needed distraction.

'Did he have an emergency that I don't know about?' she asked the dogs, pouring them some kibble from the giant bag under the sink. They wolfed it down hungrily from their bowls.

She picked up the brochure on the coffee table. It was for the Becker Institute. She sank into the couch and flicked through it absently, lingering on a photo of Jared Becker in a white coat. He was handsome, like Sebastian, smiling in a trustworthy fashion with a full set of whiter-than-white American teeth.

She considered whether he was as handsome as Sebastian. Absolutely not, she decided. Sebastian had rougher edges; he looked like he lived on an island in the sun and he looked like he loved it, too.

Where was he?

Two thin pieces of paper fell from the pages of the brochure onto the hardwood floor. Stormy made a run for them.

'Don't eat those!' Mila snatched them up as the dog went to sniff them with her wet nose.

'Tickets to Chicago on a private jet,' she told the dog aloud, realising what they were with a start. 'Sent from Jared for their mother's seventieth birthday, I suppose. One for Dr Sebastian Becker, and one for...'

She trailed off, turning the ticket over and over again, as if it might start to reveal her own name. The spare ticket was blank.

Her hands shook like jelly as she stuffed the tickets back inside the brochure and dropped it onto the table. Jared had sent him a spare open ticket. Was this plane ticket for someone else entirely? If not, why hadn't Sebastian even broached the subject of her accompanying him?

She tried his phone again. Then she tried calling the dive shop, but no one had seen or heard from him.

Panic started setting in. Annabel had left for a party on this day three years ago and never come back. They'd been having dinner when Annabel had announced she had to leave early. Some guy was waiting for her at a party.

Mila tried to fight the creeping paranoia and despair as she walked to the beach. How could he forget her, today of all days? She wasn't even particularly angry about the plane tickets, she realised. She trusted that he was hers for now at least. She just wanted to see him…to know he was safe.

A horse and cart shuttled past on the street behind her as she found a private nook behind some trees and dropped to the sand. The sound of distant music and clanging dishes mingled with the smell of barbecues and incense in the muggy air. The island was alive and the moon was bright for their planned night dive, but there was still no sign of Sebastian.

She drew her knees up, feeling anxiety form around her like a cloak.

She was back in the driveway of her mother's house now, yanking the chain off her bicycle five minutes after Annabel had left for the party. She'd been talking to her sister on the phone when the line had suddenly gone dead.

'Where are you going?' her mother had called from the driveway.

'Me and Annabel got cut off. Wait here!' she'd yelled back to her mother.

She had pedalled so hard down that road. The night had been black, the trees a frenzied mass of bare branches in the wind, and the rain had been threatening to turn from spit and drizzle into a full-blown downpour that would drench her.

But Mila had hardly felt the cold. Not from the weather anyway. She'd had a feeling. It had seeped through to this earthly plain from somewhere else and chilled her bones. *Something wasn't right with her twin sister.*

Then she'd seen the car, wrapped around a tree. She'd seen the smoke pouring from the back and from under the bonnet. She'd seen the motorbike rider, sitting in a crumpled sobbing heap at the roadside. His bike had been a twisted wreck, but the car... It hadn't even looked like a car.

And Annabel... She hadn't even looked like Annabel by the time Mila had came to her senses and tried to heave her out through the broken glass.

Mila's eyes sprang open. She couldn't go there—not again. She could have helped if only she'd been fast enough. She would never forgive herself for freezing up and wasting those precious seconds.

Mila watched the dogs sniffing around the beach for sand crabs, chasing them as if it was the greatest game in the world. If only life were so simple for humans, she thought, wading into the shallows with her lantern.

Both dogs ran over to watch as she pulled matches from her shorts pocket and lit the tiny candle at the centre of her paper lantern.

'I'm so sorry, Annabel,' she whispered as it drifted out to sea on the pull of the tide. 'I miss you so much. Please, if you're out there, send me a sign that you forgive me.'

CHAPTER THIRTEEN

MILA SLATHERED THE jasmine-scented shower gel everywhere, from her fingertips to her toes. Standing in the shower at her place, she scrubbed at her body as if she could scrub away the memories, too.

Annabel wasn't leaving her head now. The night of the accident…all that blood. And that was interspersed with her confusion and frustration over Sebastian, as if one of her nightmares had turned into the real world.

Why hadn't he called?

She was just getting started on the shampoo when the lights flickered out above her.

'Great,' she mumbled. As if the evening wasn't bad enough already, now she had to shower in the dark?

She slid down the wall to the tiled floor. Exhaustion made her bones feel heavy as she watched a yellow butterfly flit against the window outside. All those long nights of delicious sex, losing herself in Sebastian when she should have been sleeping, were taking their toll.

She let the water wash over her, trying to clear her head. They never spent time together outside, where anyone could see them. He was so concerned about her being pictured with him that they were limited to rooms with four walls and total privacy.

At first it had been kind of exciting...even though she knew it wasn't exactly sustainable. Now it was making her think that maybe he'd 'forgotten' tonight for the same reason. Maybe he didn't want to risk being seen out on another boat with her.

Mila blinked back water from her eyelashes as the lights flickered on again.

Those damn island generators.

Something strange caught her eye. The yellow butterfly was still and silent on the glass now—odd—but that wasn't it. She peered closer at the tiny red dots appearing on her bare arms. They were small and strange, blending in with the shower gel...

Wait a second. They were wriggling!

'Oh, my God!'

Mila shrieked and almost slipped as she tried

to jump clear of the water. More of the tiny red creatures were landing on her shoulders, trickling down her stomach with the shampoo trails.

Scrambling out of the shower, she grabbed up a towel and broke into a fit of sobs. She reached for the door handle just as a heavy knock on the other side made her jump out of her skin.

'Who's there?'

'Mila, it's me. Are you OK?'

She froze, trying to swallow back tears, but it was impossible.

'Mila? Let me in!'

Her body was heaving with sobs and writhing with shock and disgust—and now with utter embarrassment—but Sebastian was right there on the other side when she finally pulled the door open. He caught her in his arms as she tumbled forward in the towel. Stormy was close behind him, jumping at the doorframe.

'Mila, what's going on?'

She stayed flat against his chest in nothing but the towel, too emotional to move. Sebastian was short of breath, as if he'd run all the way here or something. His arms folded around her instantly and for a moment he just held her while she cried with the force of someone fighting to live through suffocation.

'The front door was open,' he said into her hair. 'I was looking for the dogs and for you. Mila, I'm so sorry I wasn't here for you earlier. I know what today is…'

'I'm not crying because of *you*,' she said, gathering herself together. It was partly true, at least. She forced her body to detach itself from his and pressed a palm to the bathroom door. It swung open in a cloud of hot steam. 'There are *worms* coming out of my shower!'

His brown eyes widened in horror. 'Worms?'

'Go and look,' she told him, running a shaky hand over her eyes.

She wasn't sure what had just happened, but him holding like that, just saying nothing, was making her cry even harder. He hadn't forgetten the anniversary. He'd come to look for her.

Sebastian strode purposefully into the bathroom. She heard the water still running in the shower. Then she heard him curse and turn it off. He strode back into the room, wiping his wet hands on his open blue shirt. She wanted to be touching him again.

'That's not good. It's mosquito larvae…'

'What? That wriggling red stuff is *larvae*?' Mila was repulsed. 'Are you serious?'

His broad frame dominated the room as he walked around the bed towards the door. 'It must be in the water tank. I'll get someone over here...'

'Where *were* you, Sebastian?'

She was still shaking. There was probably still soap in her hair. But Sebastian was in her bedroom after all this time. Usually they went to his place—which probably explained the larvae in her shower. She hadn't used it for a few days.

'There was an emergency,' he told her, taking her hands now, reaching one hand to her face in concern. 'I left without my phone. I meant to call...'

'I was so worried, Sebastian. I went over all the reasons why you hadn't come. You can't just tell someone you'll be somewhere and then not show up. You can't just leave... That's what Annabel did to me—three years ago on this day!'

As soon as her words were out he seemed to realise the severity of his mistake. 'Baby, I'm so sorry...'

He pulled her to the edge of the bed with him

and sat her down. She folded against him in the towel.

'It's my fault Annabel died,' she blurted. 'It's all my fault, Sebastian.'

Silence.

She sobbed into his shoulder till his shirt was wet—but she didn't care and he didn't seem to care either. His arms were still wrapped tightly around her. She had to get it all out now.

'We were on the phone while she was in the car. She was asking me about a guy. I was telling her what to do—or what *not* to do. I don't know... I can't remember. We always did that. We talked on the phone while we drove—hands-free, of course. We always had so much to say... we couldn't stop. She'd only just left the house. Then the phone went dead...'

'It's OK.' He pressed a kiss to the side of her head.

'I just had this *feeling*, like I always did.'

Her voice was as shaky as she felt, even as she tried to pull herself together for his benefit.

'I knew something was wrong. I took my bike and I found the car. There was so much blood... all coming from her...from my *sister*. I couldn't think straight. I completely froze, Sebastian.

After all my training, all my combat experience, all the times I'd rescued soldiers from burning convoys and tanks… As soon as I saw my twin sister I couldn't think of anything… Then I tried to pull her out though the windscreen. I couldn't get her through the glass, but I tried anyway. I had to do *something*. But by then I was too late. Those seconds were critical…'

'You did everything you could.'

Sebastian's gentle eyes were making her heart hurt even more.

He reached for her hands and turned her wrists over. 'Your scars,' he stated, running his thumbs along the tell-tale lines. 'They're not from Afghanistan.'

'They're from trying to pull her out of the car. But I was too late. I was just too late…'

'It wasn't your fault Annabel died, Mila.' He held her at arm's length. 'You of all people should know that. Listen to me—I cannot be the only one ever to have said this to you, but I'm going to say it again. This was *not* your fault. You need to let this go.'

He kissed her nose, her eyes and lips, then looked at her incredulously.

'That's why you didn't get plastic surgery on

your arms, isn't it? You felt like you should live with those scars because you deserved them?'

Mila couldn't even answer. He stood up from the bed. For a second she assumed he was so repulsed by her that he was leaving, but he'd picked up the long green dress from the hanger she'd hooked on the wardrobe door.

'What are you doing?' she asked him. 'We've missed the dive. And I already sent my lantern out, too.'

'Get dressed,' he commanded, holding the dress out to her. 'Come with me.'

'Agung? Can we see them?'

'Sure thing, Dr Becker. They're doing really well, in spite of… Well, you know.'

It was midnight now, but Sebastian had known Ketut and Wayan would be awake after what they had been through. The Blue Ray Clinic was quiet, but the sound of a gurgling baby made its way down the hallway as they squeaked along in their shoes.

Mila's eyes grew wide in surprise.

He hadn't told her yet.

'Is that…?'

'Come see.'

After what had happened he wanted to give Mila a surprise and make this awful night a little better—to show her exactly why he'd lost track of time and forgotten his phone.

Later he would give her the other surprise—an offer of a trip to Chicago. He'd been over the pros and cons of asking her so many times, and he'd concluded finally that he would always regret not asking her if he didn't. So he'd been saving it for tonight.

He had the plane tickets on the table...a boxed gift behind the couch... A stomach full of knots.

Agung led them through to the little recovery room which the staff had filled with balloons already.

Mila's hand flew up over her mouth. She stepped to the edge of the bed with him. 'Wayan! You had the baby!'

Wayan was beaming. 'Dr Ricci, it's so good to see you.'

'Meet baby Jack,' Sebastian said, stroking a finger across the tiny boy's cheek.

He had fallen in love with this kid already—all swathes of jet-black hair and crinkled feet and fingers...and a mouth he thought was pretty cute, even if the rest of the world might deem him in need of fixing.

'Oh, Wayan, he's beautiful.'

'Sebastian really helped us tonight,' Ketut told her, adjusting the fluffy white pillows behind Wayan. 'I called him when the contractions got too much and he brought the boat over himself… brought us back here.'

'I left my phone at the MAC when it happened,' Sebastian added.

'It's OK,' Mila told him, touching her fingers to his arm.

He put a hand on top of hers. They were supposed to have been out diving by now at Shark Reef. He was supposed to have given her the plane ticket and the gift. He'd planned it all for late evening, because he still wouldn't risk them being seen out together where anyone could take a photo of them.

Jared had laughed when he'd told him this earlier.

'You can't keep her all locked up just because of what happened with Klara, bro.'

'I'm not keeping her locked up. It's called being careful—for her protection.'

'Didn't you say she was in the Army? Does she really need your protection?'

Sure, let them all think he was paranoid…

But they hadn't seen the look on Klara's face when she'd read that letter from the parents. They hadn't seen her when her whole world fell apart. If anything like that happened to Mila—especially now she'd opened up to him about Annabel and shown she trusted him—he wouldn't forgive himself.

He knew they would have to be extremely careful in Chicago, but he considered it worth the risk to have this woman there at his side.

'I'm so happy for you,' Mila was telling Wayan and Ketut now, extending her finger to stroke the back of little Jack's hand.

The baby only went and took her finger between his tiny ones. Sebastian looked on and felt something strange…a mixture of pride for Ketut and Wayan and envy.

'You decided to join us a few weeks early, huh?' Mila whispered to Jack.

'Maybe he wanted to spend more time with Auntie Mila before she leaves the MAC?' Ketut chimed in.

'Auntie Mila… I kind of like that.' Mila smiled at Sebastian.

Sebastian reached for the cluster of balloons that had floated between them in the draught from the fan.

'Cleft lip and cleft palate, exactly as shown on the scan,' he confirmed, seeing the way Mila was studying the baby's mouth. 'Two birth defects: a right unilateral cleft lip and palate with complete deformity.'

'You'll help him, Sebastian, when the time comes,' she said conclusively.

'Of course. My team will take care of everything this little guy needs—no question,' he replied, breaking eye contact and moving the balloons to the corner of the room. His stomach had just twisted at the idea of working on Jack without her.

The trip to Chicago was to be around the same time as her flight to the UK was due. The date of her return had now been confirmed, and it remained an unspoken certainty between them. He was aware that she had things to get home to— her mother included—and asking her to meet his family was a huge decision that could change everything for them.

The media was one monster to slay, but he realised that maybe he hadn't asked her about Chicago yet because he was afraid she might say no. He was already concerned that nothing he could do would keep her in his life…that she would leave him anyway, just as Klara had.

He was totally paranoid, he concluded ruefully.

Wayan was talking again now, looking between them. Holding the baby close against her chest, she looked tired, but elated.

'No matter how many ultrasounds we saw, we couldn't really know what we would see when he arrived. I knew he would be beautiful, though, no matter what. Nothing can prepare you for the love you feel for your unborn child, Dr Ricci. And it's only intensified when it's born.'

'I can't even imagine,' Mila replied with a smile, as Ketut dropped a kiss to his wife's head.

'It's the kind of love you know you've been waiting for your whole life,' she told them, and Sebastian didn't miss the look of awe and wonder in Mila's eyes.

Was that a flicker of sadness he saw too?

CHAPTER FOURTEEN

'OPEN IT,' SEBASTIAN told her, presenting her with the long, rectangular box he'd just pulled from behind the couch.

'You're giving me gifts now?' Mila released Stormy, who had demanded a hug the second they'd walked through the villa door. 'What's this?' she asked as the dog hopped to the floor and sniffed around the couch looking for more surprises.

'Open it!'

She did as she was told, pulling the golden wrapping from the flat box, intrigued. Sebastian threw the paper to the floor, along with the huge red ribbon. Stormy pounced on it straight away, and Bruno soon joined in.

'The dress!' she exclaimed, pulling the soft, floaty light fabric from the box. 'The one from the book at the tailor's in Bali?'

It felt incredible in her hands. She was stunned, and embarrassed because it must have cost so

213213213213

much. But then she remembered he was rich. It was easy to forget, with the way he seemed to treat everyone and everything as an equal.

'I had Anya expedite it and bring it over for you.'

He took her hand and helped her off the couch and out of her wrap. She raised her arms above her head, then slowly he helped slide the dress on, until the soft blue fabric was cinched flatteringly at her waist and floating about her calves. She ran a hand along one almost transparent sleeve. Adrenaline spiked in her veins as he caught her wrist where the fabric hovered over her scars and brought it to his lips.

'It's beautiful on you,' he said, and kissed her.

He'd remembered that she liked long sleeves, to cover her scars, and even as she kissed him back Mila was mortified by the way she'd broken down in front of him earlier. It was almost two a.m. now, but her eyes were still red from crying. Bless Wayan and Ketut for not saying a word. It had been a rough day for all of them...

'Thank you,' she sighed, putting her arms around his broad shoulders. 'I love it.'

'I want to you wear it in Chicago,' he said.

Mila's heart skipped a beat as he reached down

for the brochure on the coffee table—the one she had picked up earlier.

'You're asking me to meet your family?'

'I'm asking you to accompany me to what will undoubtedly be the most lavish, over the top celebration in honour of a seventy-year-old woman you'll have ever seen. My brother and his wife Laura know how to throw a party. They've invited the entire badminton club.'

She didn't smile as she was clearly supposed to. She felt queasy. She hadn't told him she'd already seen the tickets, and she felt a little bad for jumping to conclusions about him not wanting her there.

She turned to him, still in the dress. 'I appreciate you asking me, Sebastian, but I don't think it's a good idea, do you?'

It was the honest truth. How could she go to his home with him, involve herself in his life to that extent, when they were fundamentally different at the core? She'd seen him with baby Jack. At the end of the day he wanted a family of his own here, on the island. If she went with him she would fall for him even harder. And it would only hurt her even more to lose him.

'It's just a few days in Chicago. We'll take the

helicopter to Denpasar, then it's a direct flight on the private jet. We'll have our own bedroom on board.' He kissed her passionately, ran his hands through her hair, and his words against her lips gave her tingles. 'Imagine the fun we'll have on the way...'

Mila broke away from him, imagining exactly that—the mile high club...high on each other.

The dress swished heavily around her ankles as she crossed to the doors to the garden. 'I don't know if I should be meeting your family at this point, Sebastian. I mean, I appreciate the offer, but...'

'But what? I know you need to go home and see your mother, Mila, but you can go *after* the party, can't you? And then you can come back here?'

'You mean, extend my contract at the MAC?'

'If you want.'

Her heart raced wildly. He made it all sound so simple. He was sitting there on the couch, holding the brochure and the plane tickets. The night was quiet and still, apart from the dogs, who padded past outside. Stormy was still gripping the red ribbon in her teeth.

Sebastian's jaw started to tic when he realised

she wasn't as excited as she should be, but she didn't know what to say. She was so torn.

'I want you in my life,' he said seriously. 'We're good together, Mila.'

'You won't even be seen with me in daylight!'

He wrinkled his nose. 'I wouldn't want to take you home if I didn't think you could handle what might happen there. Jared won't invite the media, so no one will take any photos we don't want them to...'

'I can't live like that, and neither should you. I'm not afraid of what people think or say about me. But that's not the point, Sebastian. I can't give you what you want—not in the long run.'

'What are you talking about?'

'A family, Sebastian. I saw the way you looked at Jack, and I see how you look when you talk about Charlie, too. I *know* that's what you want.'

Sebastian fell silent again and her cheeks flamed. She had pretty much just divulged that she'd both considered and rejected the possibility of having his children—all without him even knowing.

'This thing we have...it's complicated,' he said.

He stood up and crossed to her, and she felt his soft breath on her cheek as his strong hands found her waist from behind, urging her back against him gently.

'And I'm not asking you for anything more than your company right now,' he told her, sweeping her hair aside and dropping kisses along the nape of her neck. 'Just some time off this island together, while we figure out what's going to happen next. What do you say, Dr Ricci? You wouldn't make me listen to the badminton club gossip all alone, would you?'

CHAPTER FIFTEEN

RACHEL CAME FLYING through the MAC reception doors so fast, Mila almost mistook her for the crew bringing an emergency patient in.

'Where's Dr Becker?' Rachel asked excitedly.

Her face was beetroot-red, as if she'd run here from her villa in spite of the blazing heat. She pushed her sunglasses up to the top of her head.

'He's on the mainland again, for consultations,' Mila explained, moving out from behind the desk and closing the window on the computer screen.

She didn't want Rachel to see she'd been looking up the Beckers on the internet, in anticipation of meeting them, as well as double-checking the schedule for the day.

'He'll be back tomorrow. What's happened?'

'*This* has happened.'

Rachel fished an iPad out of her bright pink beach bag. The cover on it matched.

She stepped to Mila's side and showed her the

screen. 'It's in French, but you can see what it is,' she enthused. 'I think it's super-exciting! I know Dr Becker doesn't like photos and stuff, especially of you two...'

Mila didn't respond.

'But I think this is something different, right? I mean, it's a *kid*!'

Mila took the tablet in her hands, frowning to herself. What was she talking about? French? A kid?

She was trying not to let on, but she felt sick to the core suddenly. Was it the smell of the detergent they'd just used on the floors? Or maybe it was the eggs she'd had for breakfast? She fought to focus on the tablet. Rachel crossed her arms proudly.

Fatema walked in, and peered over Mila's shoulder. 'What are you looking at?'

'I don't even know,' Mila said, putting a hand to her stomach. 'It's in French.'

Rachel tutted and took the tablet back. 'It translates as "Breakthrough scar surgery saved my face!" It's that French kid...you know, Francoise Marchand? She got bitten by a dog. Dr Becker and Dr Ricci saved her from serious scars with his new laser treatment and now she's written this. She's only eight—can you believe it? Her story's got published in the newspaper—probably because she's so young. Kids who do cool stuff like this always get famous. I wish I was eight years old again... I would do things differently.'

She said it a little wearily, even with a hint of envy, but Mila was only half listening now. She put her hand to the back of a chair and sank slowly onto the seat—just as her next patient glided in through the doors in a full purple sarong.

'Are you OK, sweetie?'

Amita Ahluwalia's perfectly symmetrical eyebrows met in the middle as she crouched in front of her. Mila noticed the smell of the beautiful Indian model's perfume instantly.

'You've gone very pale.'

'I'm OK...don't worry,' she reassured her, swallowing back a slight gag reflex.

This was embarrassing.

'We were just showing her an exciting piece of press coverage,' Rachel explained. 'Anyone would be overwhelmed. This eight-year-old kid has written a story about her dog bite and how our new revolutionary treatment helped her heal.

It's a great testament to Dr Becker's work here. We'll get even more appointments after this. No one can resist a kid with a story... Are you OK, Dr Ricci? Do you feel sick?'

They all turned to look at her.

Mila couldn't take it any more. 'Excuse me,' she mumbled, clutching her stomach and bolting from the seat. She couldn't throw up in front of her patient, and the bathroom was just down the hall.

She heard Amita Ahluwalia's voice calling out to her to eat some charcoal as she made her dash down the hallway. Embarrassment coursed through her veins along with the nausea. She almost knocked over a vase of flowers in her hurry.

'Doctor?' Rachel was hot on her heels. 'I'm sorry if I upset you. But the article is *good*! I think Dr Becker will be OK with it. There aren't any photos of you, and it's not like you're in the same boat as his ex...'

'I don't care about that, Rachel.'

Why did everyone think she should care about that? There were far bigger things to be concerned about—like the fact that she was about to be sick at work.

Mila pushed through the door to the ladies' room and half ran, half stumbled to the toilet. With her hands on the porcelain bowl she threw up as quietly as she could—which, she realised in dismay, wasn't particularly quiet.

Rachel was in the bathroom, too. 'Dr Ricci...?'

Mila reached for the lock on the cubicle door and pulled it across. 'Please, Rachel, I'm OK—really. Nothing I can't handle. Can you just go and apologise to Miss Ahluwalia?'

She wiped at her sweaty face with her white coat sleeve, slumping back against the wall. The tiles were cold. And the lights were too bright—they were giving her a headache.

Rachel's sandals shifted beneath the door. Her voice was laced with concern now. 'Is this the first time this has happened to you?'

Mila covered her face with her hands. It was the first time she'd thrown up, but she'd been nauseous before this on a few occasions over the past few days, now that she thought about it.

'I'm... I'm sure it's nothing,' she managed.

'Go home, Dr Ricci, lie down. We'll make sure you're covered here.'

'Thank you.'

'Are you going to tell Dr Becker about this?'

'About the article?'

'No, about you being sick?'

A cold sweat prickled on her back against the tiles. 'No need to tell him anything, Rachel. Like I said, I'm OK.'

Rachel said nothing as she left the bathroom, but Mila knew what she was thinking. Her romance with Sebastian was hardly a secret around here any more. If it wasn't the floor cleaner, or the eggs… She could barely even entertain the notion of what might be causing her nausea.

'Thank you so much for agreeing to do this, Mila!'

Wayan handed over baby Jack, who was gurgling sweetly to himself. He was the epitome of cute, dressed in a little blue onesie. Then promptly put a giant padded bag laden with nappies and toys and bottles of formula over Mila's shoulder. The weight of it threatened to send her toppling sideways onto Sebastian's porch.

'Are you sure you don't mind?'

'Wayan, I told you—I love babysitting,' she enthused, straightening up with the giant bag.

She had never babysat in her life. She'd simply overheard Ketut asking Sebastian if he knew of a good babysitter, and figured it would be a chance to do something nice for the couple while Sebastian was away on the mainland. She also hoped spending some time with little Jack would help her relax, and think things through.

She eyed the paper bag on the dining table, feeling her throat dry up. There was something else she had to do, too…

'You guys just go and enjoy your dinner,' she said to Wayan, plastering a smile onto her face as the dressed-up woman gave her son an extra kiss on his chubby cheek.

Stormy and Bruno bounded ahead of her into the house and, carrying baby Jack under her arm, Mila made herself some tea. It wasn't the easiest thing, holding a baby… But she was doing fine, she told herself, nothing to worry about here.

The paper bag on the table seemed to be calling her.

Take the test! You know it's going to be negative! Just put your mind at rest!

She would do it later. Maybe even tomorrow.

Right now she would continue her research on the Beckers. She might even watch an episode of *Faces of Chicago* and see what all the fuss was about.

She would do anything, she realised quickly, other than take the damn test.

Jack snoozed on the couch next to her as she scrolled through Francoise's article on Sebastian's spare iPad. The kid had written some really sweet things about the MAC and her time on the island, and how she was proud to have been brave like Dr Mila Ricci.

Mila couldn't deny that she was proud to be part of the story. She hoped Sebastian would be proud, too. It wasn't anything close to the kind of 'publicity' that vultures like Hugo O'Shea liked to print. This was only drawing attention to the positive impact his work was having on the island and their patients.

The sharp, shrill ringtone of her phone woke the sleeping baby. He coughed and then started screaming like a banshee. She had never heard a sound quite like it. She bundled him onto her lap and held him close, rocking him.

'No, no, no…it's OK, Jack. I'm sorry.'

Jack's shrieks of discomfort burrowed under her skin, filling her with dread, as a yellow butterfly flitted in through the open door and came to a stop on the arm of the couch. It sat there even as she reached past it for her phone, to decline the call.

Sebastian. She would have to call him back. She couldn't talk to him when Jack was crying like this.

Something maternal seemed to take control of her body as she rocked and whispered and cooed. 'There you go...you're doing fine, little man.'

But Jack cried and cried, and Mila contemplated singing to him.

What did babies *want*?

She had no clue, but the way he smelled was heavenly. Did all babies smell this nice? His skin was so clear and bright around his little misshapen mouth, and she loved the way his all-seeing eyes shone when he wasn't screaming. He'd have an idyllic life here...seeing the ocean every day, diving in it with his godfather, Sebastian. It must be an incredible privilege to watch a little person grow, to know you'd influenced their life decisions.

She felt a familiar dread creep in again, even as Jack fell silent in her arms. She liked the idea of it...but then she remembered why she wasn't cut out for motherhood—that she'd be terrible at it.

It was all her friends at home who wanted to

be mothers, and her mum would've loved to be a grandma, and Sebastian… They all wanted the babies—not her.

Speaking of Sebastian, she should call him back.

Anything to put off taking the test.

CHAPTER SIXTEEN

SEBASTIAN WAS SEATED at a chequered-cloth-covered table between two potential investors who were keen to know more about his plans for the villa complex in the valley. Their waiter was already delivering plates of seafood pasta to their Italian-themed place mats.

'Dr Ricci?' He answered the voice call when the vibration in his pocket didn't stop. 'I have to be fast—I'm in a restaurant. Is everything OK over there?'

Her face flashed onto the screen just as one of his investors peered at it over his spaghetti.

'So this is Dr Ricci? The little French girl painted a wonderful picture of you in her article, but look at you—you're even more delightful in person. Whose baby do you have there?'

'Baby?' Sebastian realised that baby Jack was there, swaddled in a fluffy grey blanket next to Mila. His own *Chicago* shirt was still draped across the cushions on the couch behind her, where he'd left it.

'You're babysitting?' he said in surprise.

The investors were taking in Jack's cleft lip, witnessing Mila with the baby at the same time as him.

'It's my godson,' he explained. He probably shouldn't have picked up her video call—this wasn't looking too professional right now. But he'd thought she would be at the MAC. Mixing business with pleasure was risky...

'What's wrong with his face?' one of them asked.

'He has a cleft lip and palate. I'll be operating in a couple months or so—'

'He's so good, though,' Mila cut in. 'It's almost like he knows Dr Becker is going to help him— so he's being very brave, aren't you, sweetie?'

They all watched as she cuddled him close. Sebastian had never seen her like this. The investors looked truly touched for a moment, and a sudden rush of pride swept over him for both Mila and for Jack.

'Seems you're very close with your staff and your patients,' one of the investors observed. 'Do you open your home to them all like this?'

'Not at all.' Sebastian cleared his throat. 'But things are certainly different on the island. Excuse me just a second…?'

He inched his way past the chairs and tables and the harried waiters, through a waft of parmesan cheese to the door. Outside the air was thick and muggy, reminding him that he was actually still in Bali—not Italy.

'Sorry about that,' he said to Mila. 'I called you earlier to say I should be back by tomorrow, but I need to stay here another night with these investors. I can't get into the base facility till morning and I want to show them around.'

'So the investors have read the article by Francoise?'

He told her he'd been forced to read young Francoise's story that morning, and while he could hardly be angry at the kid for singing his praises, it was a little irritating, putting it in some French newspaper without his consent. More than irritating. Sure, there were no photos of him with Mila, and it wasn't a 'celebrity scandal' angle at all, but the publicity still drew attention where attention wasn't needed.

'Not all press is bad press,' Mila reminded him. 'Sebastian, you have to be OK with people writing things about you if it's done with good intentions. You're doing great work—you deserve to be recognised.'

'Thank you,' he told her sincerely. 'It's sexy when you put me in my place.'

She laughed.

Mila hadn't experienced the extent of the media's wrath enough to appreciate why he despised any hint of attention on him, but he was grateful for her indifference about such things—it was refreshing. It kind of calmed him down.

He told her how these investors from Jakarta were interested in his project there on the mainland. They loved the outside space, the funicular and the villas. They saw incredible potential *and* they were excited.

'I'd prefer Jared to get on board too,' he added quietly. 'He had some great ideas when we talked about it… But I have no choice except to move forward now. There are too many people who can't afford the MAC—we need facilities in both places. So the sooner we can get things moving the better.'

'You love creating more work for yourself, don't you?' she teased him.

He grinned. 'It's how I thrive.'

He turned back to the restaurant, saw the two investors toasting each other through the window. He knew they were likely congratulating themselves on getting involved, even if they hadn't signed anything yet. It was a good sign, he supposed. And he had Mila to thank for this. She had made a lasting impression on Francoise. And vice versa.

'Is everything else OK?' he asked her. 'I should really get back to them.'

Mila looked torn for a moment. She opened her mouth to speak, but then seemed to think better of it. 'Nothing that can't wait,' she said finally.

'You sure?'

'Quite sure.'

He took in the sight of her with baby Jack just for a moment longer before hanging up. She might only want a dog in her family in the future, but it hadn't escaped his attention that she looked pretty hot with a baby.

The clear blue line seemed to darken ominously as Mila studied it from the toilet seat. She was trembling ferociously and her head reeled in the candlelit outdoor bathroom. The crickets seemed to be singing into the night, taunting her from behind the stone wall.

How was this possible? *It couldn't be possible.* She'd been taking her pill the whole time—at the right time.

She would do another test.

Panic strangled her heart as she made her way back to Jack. He was still snoozing soundly, swaddled in his blanket. It seemed so telling, somehow, that the test should come up positive while she was babysitting.

Annabel flashed into her mind. She dropped to the floor beside the couch. She had asked for a sign on the night of the anniversary. Maybe this was Annabel's sign that she'd forgiven her for the accident and was encouraging her to start a family. Stranger things had happened, right?

Mila scowled at the floor, dragging her hands through her hair. She was being ridiculous. This wasn't some divine message from the other side—this was her own fault. She had probably forgotten to take her pill one night, or taken it too late.

You love him. This is the right thing for you.

The voice was in her head, but somehow it came from somewhere else. Mila spun around to Jack. His eyes were open and he was gazing up at the ceiling from the cushions.

Getting to her feet, she put her finger to his little hand, but he didn't stop looking at the ceiling, as if he was seeing something that wasn't there.

'What are you doing, little man?' she whispered, trying not to feel spooked.

Tears prickled her eyes. She wouldn't speak to her twin sister. She wasn't in this room. Annabel was gone and Sebastian had made her feel it was OK to let her go, to forgive herself for not being able to help when she'd still had time.

She rarely had nightmares about Annabel any more—in fact, she'd only had a few since she'd started sleeping in Sebastian's bed—but of course she was still in her every thought. She was part of her.

'We always said we'd have babies at the same time,' she said aloud. What was the harm in talking to her just for a bit...just in case? 'But by no means was an accidental pregnancy ever on the cards—especially one that's the result of a fling with an ex-celebrity doctor from Chicago. You would tell me off, if you were here, Annabel.'

You love him. This is the right thing for you.

She heard it again, loud and clear.

Mila shook her head at herself, petting Stormy when she padded over for some attention.

'Good girl,' she said softly when the dog pressed her nose to Jack's little foot.

She sat there in silence as Jack drifted off to sleep again.

What to do?

She couldn't ask anyone at the clinic to test her for pregnancy—it would have to be another kit. It had been tough enough getting the first one from the storeroom without anyone seeing her.

If anyone even suspected she was pregnant they would know without a doubt that Sebastian was the father. It wasn't ideal, showing up as his employee and leaving pregnant with his baby. Besides, he hated attention—and people would surely fix their attention on *this* juicy piece of scandal.

What would he say when she told him, if the second test came back positive too? Would he want this baby with her? And if he did…what if something happened to it?

This was everything she'd been afraid of and all of it was unbearable to contemplate.

'Help me through this, Annabel,' she begged out loud, in spite of herself. 'I don't think I can do this on my own.'

CHAPTER SEVENTEEN

Two weeks later

'WHERE'S THAT NICE female surgeon who was here for the initial consultation?'

The fifty-six-year-old British woman blinking up at Sebastian was nervous without Mila there for her blepharoplasty.

'She had to leave unexpectedly this morning,' he explained, reaching behind him to the gramophone to lay the needle on the vinyl. Beethoven filled the room and he thought of Mila. He hoped she was all right.

'Nothing serious, I hope?'

His patient's eyes were full of genuine concern and so were Fatema's. Mila had clearly touched their patient on some deeper level, in the brief time they'd been in contact, just as she had Francoise.

'Dr Ricci was truly encouraging,' his patient was saying to them now, taking Fatema's arm.

'She said I didn't need this. She said that lines around our eyes are proof of all the times we've smiled, and the more we smile the more beautiful we are to everyone who sees us. Isn't that a nice thing to say? She could have just tried to sell me more plastic surgery.'

'That's not really our policy here,' Sebastian told her, fighting a smile.

It sounded as if Mila had made an even bigger impression that he'd thought. This was the sort of thing he'd been hearing ever since Mila had arrived at the MAC: *'Mila is so wonderful...'* *'Mila is so caring...'* *'Mila is so good for you... we mean, good for the MAC.'*

Shame she'd left the MAC earlier on today, saying she felt sick.

He was used to the gossip about them by now, of course, and he didn't care about that as long as their photos weren't splashed about the internet. It still gave him chills to think about how it had ended with Klara, and with Mila still set to come to Chicago with him for his mother's birthday party there was always the chance that someone would stick a lens where it wasn't wanted and make things difficult.

He was praying it would all go smoothly. She

was well aware he wanted her to stay on at the MAC for various reasons, but they'd agreed that spending some time away from the island to talk about things would be the best course of action before putting it officially on paper.

It was the right thing to do. She had come on board as a temporary employee after all. Neither of them had expected this, and they couldn't exactly keep it a secret with the island itself more like a gossip factory than his last surgery in Chicago, just with more sand and fewer cameras.

Fatema cornered him when he went for the anti-bac. 'Is Mila still sick, then?' she asked him.

'Dr Ricci? I guess so… Maybe she ate something bad.'

'Like before?' Fatema seemed concerned. 'She needs to watch her diet.'

'Before? What do you mean?' He shook the anti-bac from the bottle, then handed it to her.

Fatema looked sheepish. She turned her back to their patient and lowered her voice. A couple of weeks ago—she was sick then, too. I think you were away in Bali. She didn't tell you?'

'Why would she tell me?'

Fatema cocked an eyebrow. 'We *all* know why she would tell you, Dr Becker.'

He grunted. 'Fine. But, no, she didn't tell me.'

The information nagged at his brain even as he forced himself to return to the task at hand. He should be focusing on the fact that he oversaw the most capable and qualified team in Indonesia, instead of wondering if Mila's strange moods and impromptu sick leave were something he should worry about.

She had been sick before today and not told him…?

Fatema was talking to their patient about the procedure. 'So, just to recap, Dr Ricci must have told you to avoid taking any medication that might thin your blood and prevent it from clotting normally prior to this surgery?'

'Yes, Dr Halabi, she explained all that.'

'That includes pain relievers, aspirin and ibuprofen. I trust you stopped those too? And you've only eaten very lightly today, if at all?'

'Dr Ricci told me not to have breakfast or drink anything after midnight the night before my procedure. So I had no margaritas last night—which was such a shame because they were buy-one-get-one-free.'

'You can make up for that later,' Sebastian interjected.

'She also said not to wear make-up—hence this mess you see here before you.'

His patient gestured to her plain face and mascara-free eyes, but he left the make-up chat to Fatema. She was more than capable of handling this.

He couldn't help replaying in his mind an episode from earlier in the week, when he'd taken Mila out on the dive boat. She'd gone for the ride, but she hadn't wanted to dive.

'You don't want to go down?' he'd asked her. 'I was kidding about the sharks. There won't be any sharks, but the manta rays around here—they're something else!'

'I think I'm just liking the feeling of the sun on my skin right now,' she'd told him distractedly.

He'd gone down with the group without her, but he hadn't been able to fully switch off as he usually did.

Mila was being quieter than usual, less involved. Just as she'd been after they'd first kissed, back when she'd pushed him away because she'd thought he'd hooked up with Annabel. She was supposed to be diving with the group tonight, but she'd already told him she couldn't go. He hadn't questioned it because he'd seen she clearly wasn't feeling one hundred percent.

He frowned as Fatema talked details to their patient with exemplary confidence. Mila always went quiet when she had something on her mind. Maybe she was just a little nervous about meeting his family, he mused. They were set to leave tomorrow, so he could understand that. His family could be difficult to handle.

Or maybe she was nervous about finishing her placement at the MAC with nothing set in stone for the future. He couldn't help mulling over that one himself. He hadn't and wouldn't put any extra pressure on her, but the thought of being here without Mila weighed heavy on his heart.

Mila woke from the dream with a jump. She flung her legs over the side of the bed, grabbed the cool pillow beside her and pressed her hot face to the cotton. Thank goodness Sebastian wasn't there—although his comforting arms would be a relief to sink into right now.

In the dream she'd been holding a baby on her lap in a car, but there hadn't been any seatbelts. She'd been forced to travel anyway, as the base camp wasn't safe. They'd been in convoy, cruising by night across the desert plains, taking bumpy secret routes that didn't even exist in reality, dodging insurgents like characters in a video game.

Then the car had been hit—attacked from behind by Afghan soldiers with larger than life AK-47s. The bullets had rained down through the roof and the windscreen and when she'd cried out, begging for the baby's life, the baby had been gone. Vanished.

She'd woken up hotter than fire, still shaking.

Somehow she made it to the bathroom, ran the cold tap and splashed her face. Thank goodness someone had been in to clear the mosquito larvae from the tank, but there were other things wriggling under her skin now: the second test had come back positive and her dreams had returned with a vengeance. They even had a new twist to torture her with.

She studied her face in the mirror as shame washed over her. Would Sebastian comfort her if he knew what she was hiding? It had taken her several days to build up the courage to take the second test, and she still hadn't told Sebastian she was pregnant.

She hadn't told anyone.

The time difference might be a blessing in one way. It would be a good time to talk to her mother in the UK. Surely she could tell her mother?

No. She couldn't tell her—not on the phone anyway.

Every time she so much as thought about telling her mother it became more real in her head. And the more real the baby was for her, the harder it would be to lose it. And she would lose it, surely—because she wasn't a suitable mother. She couldn't care for a baby as a baby needed to be cared for. She just...*couldn't*.

Mila pulled on a T-shirt and shorts. She slipped into her flip-flops and left the room, heart pounding. It was almost five a.m. She realised she was holding her belly protectively as she walked, looking out for dogs that might attack, and when she caught herself doing it she forced her hands away.

She was already looking out for this baby when she didn't even know if she could keep it.

She hadn't been diving, even though she'd wanted to, but Sebastian had gone diving again last night. She'd made another excuse, which she'd felt terrible about. He was worried about her, she could tell. She'd simply told him she would see him the next day. It had bought her more time, but it had brought her nightmares, too.

She had no clue how he'd react to her news, but she had to tell him. The secret was killing her.

It was only the gardener out at this hour, raking leaves from the pathways, and she squared her shoulders at Sebastian's gates and psyched herself up to let herself in. Her legs felt like jelly.

As usual, the dogs greeted her as if she'd just come home from war.

'Hey, Stormy. Hey, Bruno. Oh, it's good to see you, too.'

Sebastian's suitcase was still on the porch—the one he'd half packed for Chicago. He'd spilled milk on it, thanks to Stormy, and left it by the hammock to dry. Just the sight of it made her feel sicker. She'd put this off for so long that they were due to leave tonight and she still hadn't told him.

Was she crazy? She wasn't usually the kind of person who had difficulty speaking up; in fact, the strength to do that had defined her entire career. Why was this any different? You just said it and then it was out…just like the way she'd told him about the car crash that had killed Annabel. Eventually.

But it was so hard.

Maybe she should tell him once they'd left the island. When they'd have more space and time to talk things through privately. That was what they were due to be doing anyway—he wanted her to come back here with him, didn't he, after Chicago? He had told her as much.

He just wasn't anticipating an unplanned baby with the package, Mila!

She stepped up to the porch, but she could tell Sebastian wasn't home. Her instincts kicked in.

There must have been an emergency.

CHAPTER EIGHTEEN

'IS SHE GOING to be OK?'

Pedro's eyes were tired and full of panic, and he'd bitten his fingernails almost down to the cuticles. The twenty-eight-year-old from Brazil hadn't left the Blue Ray Clinic or the decompression chamber room all night. He was still wearing his wetsuit. So was Sebastian, under his white coat.

'The team will keep an eye on her, but we've done everything we can up to this point,' Sebastian said, taking the coffee an intern had handed him and peering through the circular window at Pedro's girlfriend, Rose. 'We'll know more when the tests come back.'

What a crazy night. He was utterly exhausted, but he felt it was his duty to stay with the guy; he'd been down there on the dive with him when it had happened. He was glad Mila hadn't gone with them in the end—things hadn't exactly gone to plan.

Pedro's girlfriend, twenty-seven-year-old Rose, had panicked over something under the water at fifteen metres down. He still wasn't sure what it had been, but there had been nothing the team could do to stop her as she'd pushed her way up to the surface without a safety stop. They always did a safety stop at five meters…

'Sebastian?'

Mila's voice made him spin around—Pedro, too. She looked as dazed as he felt. For a moment, in his deep fatigue, he almost went to wrap his arms around her, but he stopped himself. 'Dr Ricci, good morning.'

'Can I see you outside?'

He excused himself and took her out of the room into the hallway, shutting the door behind him. Agung and the resident intern threw them a look, but he signalled with his coffee as if it was perfectly normal to be standing with Mila in his wetsuit at six a.m. in the Blue Ray Clinic's hallway.

'Good *morning*?' she said, lowering her voice to a whisper. She looked him up and down. 'You haven't been to bed, Sebastian.'

'That girl has been in the decompression chamber since we brought her in from the dive.'

Mila looked horrified. 'The dive you were on last night?'

He nodded, noting her pink toenails in her flip-flops. 'We had to call the air ambulance from Lombok to get her back—she might not have made it on the boat. She's still out with decompression sickness… What are you doing here so early?'

Mila's face was pale, he noticed. She was watching the cleaner with her mop and bucket at the other end of the hall, and covering her mouth with her hand.

'Are you feeling sick again?' he asked, resisting the urge to put a hand to her cheek.

She averted her eyes. 'I'm not feeling sick. This is just awful, Sebastian—are *you* OK?'

Sebastian hadn't realised till she'd said it that he probably *wasn't* entirely OK. It was really rare for something like this to happen. It was shocking, to say the least, and he'd been running on adrenaline all night.

'I wasn't her dive buddy—that was Pedro, her boyfriend,' he told her, resting a foot against the wall behind him and tapping the bottom of his coffee cup. 'But we were all there. There were six of us. I guess that's one good thing—we managed to help her pretty fast after she came up.'

'I'm so sorry this happened.'

Mila was studying his face as if she was looking for signs that he might crack. Of course he wouldn't crack, but her eyes were so full of concern. He couldn't remember the last time any woman had cared this deeply about his well-being.

'You must be so tired. We can talk later. I'll let you get back to Pedro.'

She made to turn around, but he caught her arm. 'Wait. What did you want to talk to me about so early in the morning?'

She paused, half with her back to him. She was still looking at the cleaner's mop and bucket as if it was causing her physical pain.

'Mila?'

'Dr Becker?' The obstetrician, Dr Raya, had exited the room opposite. 'Rose's tests are back. Do you have a moment?'

He looked at Mila. 'You can talk to us both,' he said quickly, following Dr Raya back into the room.

Mila had crossed her arms beside him as they waited. Dawn was breaking outside and he could hear the ocean close by through the open window. It didn't calm him down. He was on high alert now—he could tell something was wrong.

Dr Raya looked him right in the eyes and took a long, deep breath. 'Dr Becker, Dr Ricci... The tests show your patient Rose was pregnant. I don't think she knew, as neither she nor her boyfriend mentioned it, I believe?'

Sebastian shook his head gravely as Mila walked over to the window, wrapping her arms around herself. This was not what he'd hoped to hear. 'Pedro didn't mention it, no. Poor guy.'

'Poor Rose,' Mila croaked, metres away now.

'It was four to five weeks, but I'm afraid with the decompression...'

'There's no chance of a pregnancy surviving,' he finished, tossing his coffee cup into the rubbish bin under the desk, hard. 'Damn—could this night get any worse?'

He shoved his hands into his white coat pockets, fists clenched. 'We should tell Pedro, so he can prepare himself before Rose wakes up. We don't want to distress her any more than necessary. She might need a few more sessions in the decompression chamber, so he'll have to decide when to let her know.'

Mila was shifting on her feet now, holding a hand to her mouth again. Before he or Dr Raya could say anything she raced from the window right past them, yanked open the door and stepped into the hallway.

He followed her halfway to the reception area her before she threw up—right into the cleaner's bucket.

Mila was mortified. It was that smell again. If it hadn't been for the smell she might have avoided throwing up—but she couldn't think about it again, she was far too humiliated.

'You should go back inside to Pedro,' she heard herself say as the sea breeze outside caught her hair, cooling her down.

Sebastian had ushered her out, past the stunned cleaner and several patients already in Reception.

'You were the one diving with him—he should hear this news from you.'

'I know,' he said, darkly.

She sat down on the wall outside the Blue Ray Clinic in the shade of a palm tree. It was getting lighter by the second and she felt even more exposed now he was standing in front of her, arms folded.

'You want to tell me what's going on?'

She considered her regrettable timing. This was not the time or place—especially with poor Rose in there in the decompression chamber and her poor boyfriend Pedro about to learn she'd lost a baby he hadn't even know she was expecting.

It was the worst time to tell him she was carrying a baby of her own, and she felt guilty. Why should *she* be pregnant when Rose…?

'Mila, Fatema told me you were sick before… when I was in Bali. Now this?'

Sebastian crouched down to her level. He still had his wetsuit on under his white coat, she realised. He hadn't slept all night and now he was here, trying to take care of her.

It was all too much. Above everything else she despised feeling so trapped and vulnerable; this wasn't who she was.

'And you wouldn't come diving. I mean, I'm happy you didn't come last night—don't get me wrong. Accidents happen, but you never expect a dive student to dismiss every single thing she's learnt in the face of panic…'

He trailed off when he realised what he'd said.

His face said it all, though. He blamed Rose for what had happened—just as she still blamed herself for Annabel.

She needed to get away. She needed to be alone.

But Sebastian was holding her hand tight to her own lap. 'Talk to me.'

'I don't know what to say, Sebastian. It's the worst possible time.'

He stood up again. 'You're pregnant, aren't you?'

The world seemed to go white around her. How did he know…? *He's a doctor—that's how*, she told herself wearily.

'Mila? Are you pregnant?'

She still couldn't speak. Instead she just nodded and covered her face for a moment, taking deep breaths. She felt as if she might pass out.

'My God. You are.'

Sebastian sounded devastated and it made her heart ache. If she hadn't already thrown up, she might have done it again.

He turned towards the mountains and watched an early-morning horse trot past with a cart-load of boxes full of beer. This was surreal. She felt as she was looking at herself from outside her own body, hearing someone else saying these things about another person.

'I'm so sorry... I didn't know how to tell you before. It's not exactly something I planned—it's not even what I want...'

'How long have you known?'

'Two weeks.'

'Two *weeks*?' He kicked up the sand at his feet in frustration, then appeared to regret it, but he looked less than happy when he turned back to her. 'You've known for a whole fortnight and you didn't tell me? Mila, we're about to go and see my family—when exactly were you planning to tell me this? This involves me too, doesn't it?' He narrowed his eyes. 'It *is* mine, right?'

'Of course it's yours!' she exclaimed hotly.

'Then when were you going to let me in on this?'

'Today. Now.'

The disappointment on his face at her secrecy brought a lump to her throat. She knew she deserved it, but she felt cold as she struggled for composure. 'I thought we could talk about it when we'd left the island. I realise in retrospect that wasn't the best decision on my part—'

'I have to go deal with Pedro,' he said, cutting her off.

'OK.'

She watched helplessly as he rubbed his tired eyes, a foot away from her. 'We'll talk about this when I'm done. Will you be OK getting back to the house?'

She nodded mutely. Of course she would.

But her heart sank to the pit of her stomach as he strode purposefully back inside without another word. He was furious with her. He would probably end things between them now, seeing as she had basically just taken a firearm to his trust.

Her mind was a running commentary of self-loathing as she hurried back to his house. She needed to cuddle the dogs or something.

She should have told him sooner. She should *not* have told him today, when he'd had no sleep and had something pressing to deal with. Now she'd have to sit on a plane with him, meet his family, with this hanging over them… If he even still wanted her to go with him.

This was all too much. She had to get off this island—think about things rationally and logically somewhere no one could influence her decisions. Not even him.

Mila turned around and made for her consulting room instead. She'd forgotten to tell Personnel to cancel her transfer to the UK because Jared had organised the Chicago trip—she still had her ticket back to Gatwick.

CHAPTER NINETEEN

'WE DIDN'T EVEN know she was pregnant, otherwise we wouldn't have gone diving.' Pedro was slumped over on the leather couch under the ceiling fan with his head between his knees.

'I'm so sorry to have to tell you,' Sebastian said, wringing his hands together on the chair opposite.

He was too exhausted to process anything properly—too sleep-deprived to think about anything beyond the answers to Pedro's questions: *'What happened to the baby? How many more sessions will she need in there? Should we even tell her she was pregnant? Does she need to know? Won't that upset her more?'*

It was almost inconceivable that he was breaking this tragic news to Pedro, hearing him contemplate such a personal dilemma, when he'd just found out about Mila's pregnancy.

What would he do in Pedro's shoes?

He would tell his partner—he knew he would. But Mila hadn't spoken to him about anything. She'd left it *two weeks* before telling him. And she'd been reluctant even then.

Pedro's phone rang.

'I think I can take over here,' Dr Raya said kindly, taking Sebastian aside. 'You were up all night, Dr Becker, and I'm sure this has been pretty shocking for you, too. And poor Dr Ricci... I hope she gets better soon.'

Dr Raya had offered to help Pedro break the news to Rose about her pregnancy—because of course Rose should know. It was important information. Wasn't it? Someone being pregnant? All parties involved deserved to know.

Instead of going straight back to the house, he went to the rocks off the bay where he'd sat with Mila the night of the fundraiser. He was feeling emotional after last night and because of Pedro's situation. He didn't want to take that out on Mila any more than he already had. He was furious that she'd kept such a secret—he wouldn't deny that—but maybe he was more angry at himself for not noticing the signs.

He should have picked up on her pregnancy. He should have known what was happening right in front of him. He was a doctor, for crying out loud. How could he have been so blind?

He'd been too caught up in their relationship... He hadn't felt this way about anyone before—not even Klara, he realised with a jolt—and now this.

Guilt crept its way in with the sea breeze as he made his way back from the rocks barefoot, relishing the occasional stab of coral to wake him up.

When he'd snapped at Mila before he'd been in total shock. It had been pure self-defence on his part, a grappling for control. He hadn't had the capacity to process everything that was going on and he'd freaked out.

It wasn't as if either of them had been expecting this. This was an accident...

He fixed his stare on the shadows drifting across the mountains. He still couldn't wrap his head around the fact she hadn't told him.

Was it because she really didn't want a baby?

They'd joked about how she would rather have a dog, but he liked to think he knew her better now. Mila was always going to be cut up about Annabel, which meant she was always going to be scared about losing anyone close to her.

She didn't think he knew her at all, but he did.

* * *

'Mila?'

Sebastian took the porch steps in one jump with the dogs at his heels. The house was still locked up. It didn't even look as if she'd been inside.

'Damn,' he cursed as he almost fell over his suitcase, right where he'd left it himself.

He wheeled it inside with him, sweat sticking his wetsuit to his back. He was so tired… He hadn't finished packing for Chicago…he hadn't even had time to get changed.

'Don't make me spill anything else on this— I need it,' he said sternly to Stormy, who was sniffing the case as if it was loaded with ice-cream.

The dog wagged her tail and cocked her head. He wondered what it must be like to think only thoughts of food and love all day—certainly a hell of a lot less complicated than being a human.

'Mila!' he called again, dumping the suitcase on the bed.

She wasn't in the upstairs bathroom. She wasn't anywhere.

He pulled out his phone. No missed calls. He kicked off his shoes and heaved himself out of the wetsuit. He needed a shower badly, but he barely even registered being under the water when he stepped into it.

He was mad at himself for the way he'd acted earlier. Why *would* she call him?

He would check her place next...

'Mila!'

He went to knock on her door, then caught himself. He checked in every single direction for anyone who might have followed him with a camera, then pounded it with a fist. His hair was still wet from the shower. A woman passed by and eyed him up and down.

'I know her,' he explained. 'Mila, come out— we need to talk.'

He shot to the window and peered inside. 'No, no, no, no.... Are you kidding me?'

Her bedroom was practically empty. There were barely any clothes left on the hangers she always kept on the wardrobe doors instead of inside it. He loved it that she did that. The dresser was empty, too. Nothing but the hair dryer that had been there before she'd moved in.

When he called her it went straight to voicemail.

He set off at a jog, in the direction of the dive

shop. She might have moved to a hotel—somewhere more private, he thought, trying to think of some logical explanation. She might have gone to another part of the island, where she wouldn't have to be around the MAC.

But why would she do that?

They were supposed to be leaving for Chicago in a matter of hours.

He was starting to get a very bad feeling. She had packed all her bags...she hadn't said goodbye...

His phone buzzed, hot in his pocket.

'Mila?' he answered, without checking.

He stopped at the beach shack, sank to a stool in the shade. Someone he knew offered him a coconut and he accepted it gratefully.

'Dr Becker? It's Ava in Personnel—is everything all right?'

His human resources manager and all-round star player. 'Ava? What's going on?'

'Maybe you can tell me...' Ava sounded confused. 'I just had a check-in announcement come through on my email. Dr Ricci has checked in at the airport in Denpasar. Something didn't strike me as right, though. I thought I'd heard her say a while ago that she was going to void the ticket and go to Chicago first.'

264 ENTICED BY HER ISLAND BILLIONAIRE

Sebastian dug his straw hard into the coconut flesh and swivelled the stool away from the bar. No one should see his face right now.

'I'll deal with this—thank you, Ava,' he said.

Amelia Ricci's face was a picture of confusion as she flung the front door open seconds after Mila had stepped wearily from a taxi. It was so cold in Rye...the hedges round the lawn were bald. She wasn't used to it.

'Mila, what are you doing here? My God, you must be freezing.'

Mila felt numb inside and out as she was bundled into her mother's soft cardigan-clad arms. She couldn't cry...she'd run out of tears—or at least she'd thought so, until she smelled the scent of her childhood.

'I've missed you, Mum.'

Mila crumpled into the familiar warmth. She had missed this. Even though she had felt this sense of home in Sebastian's arms until she'd messed it all up.

'I think I've done something really stupid, Mum.'

'What's happened?'

Her mother ushered them both inside, wrapped

a green woollen blanket around Mila's shoulders and placed her on the sofa. She sank back against the cushions with the elephant covers on—the ones Annabel had brought back from India one time.

'Mila, are you hurt?'

She'd only just realised she was crying again.

'No, I'm not hurt, Mum. I'm pregnant. It's Sebastian's.'

Her mother's hand found hers and grasped it tight. Then she wrapped her arms around her again and held her for a long time.

'It's OK…that's not the end of the world. Here, take your jacket off…'

'I told him—or rather he guessed—and then he freaked out because I'd kept it a secret. I don't want to lose him because of this, but I can't do it.'

'What can't you do?'

Her mother helped her remove her leather jacket, sleeve by sleeve, she was too weak at this point.

'My goodness, look how tanned you are!'

'I can't have a baby, Mum.'

Her mother tutted, shook her head. 'Mila, you *can* have a baby. You're already pregnant.'

Mila took a cushion and pushed a strangled noise out into an elephant. 'It was an accident.'

'But you do you want this baby with him?'

'I don't know... Yes... I shouldn't have left without talking to him properly...it's absolutely the worst way to hurt him. I tried to call him when I got off the plane but his phone's turned off. He's probably halfway to Chicago by now.'

'Chicago?' Her mother placed a hand to her knee.

'I was supposed to go there with him to meet his family.'

'So this is serious? With Sebastian?'

Mila offered a non-committal shrug, but the depth of what she'd done and how she felt was really sinking in now. She might have just run away from the best thing ever to have happened to her.

'Listen, I'm going to make us some tea and then we can talk about this.'

Mila watched her mother fuss around the kitchen through bleary eyes. She must look such a mess—she hadn't slept at all on the plane. She'd sat there listening idly to meditation podcasts, feeling terrible after her snap decision, which she'd made when she'd been in fight-or-flight mode. She hadn't expected the regret to start as soon as the plane took off.

She grimaced into the cushion. She had gone without talking to him first. Just like his ex, Klara, had done. They'd barely ever talked about her—it was a moot point for the most part, because Mila had been able to see he'd moved on… with *her.*

But she knew him well enough by now. She'd been trained to read his body language. His moods had used to darken whenever Klàra's name had come up. Her departure and subsequent refusal to talk to him had devastated him, and now *she* had done exactly the same thing.

CHAPTER TWENTY

THE TOURISTS AT the gift shops, the queue for business class… It would usually have been torture. But Sebastian had somehow succeeded in zoning out the drone of chatter and the beeps of loud speakers. If people took photos of him he didn't notice, but he waited till he was checked in and standing by the window in the departure lounge to call Jared.

'I can't come to Chicago. Something's come up.'

He explained the situation as best he could, told him Mila was pregnant and that it wasn't planned, that he had to go and make things right.

He wanted to. He'd booked the next flight out to London. He figured if he could get to her maybe she would listen to him before she decided on anything too rash.

'This is crazy, brother!' Jared was confounded. 'Do you love this woman? I mean, *really* love her enough to have a kid with her?'

'I do—absolutely.'

Jared let out the longest sigh down the phone. 'Then we'll miss you at the party. So will Mom. We have some news for you that would've been better given in person. But I support you.'

Sebastian didn't need his support on this—not that he would tell his brother that.

He'd asked for Jared's opinion once before, when Klara had left him. Brother to brother, Jared had advised him not to go after her—not to fly over to Thailand, or Kathmandu, or any of the other places she'd gone to teach after humiliation had forced her to abort all form of contact with him. So Sebastian had let her go...until he'd missed her too much.

Then he'd flown to all those places, searching for her—of course he had. He'd just never told anyone. It had been a regrettable set of moves, on reflection. Klara had refused to see him in any of those places either.

Luckily he'd fallen in love with Gili Indah while he'd been flying out from Bali every weekend to try and find her, until eventually he'd never left the island at all—not to look for her, anyway. He'd made a life there at the MAC, he was needed and respected on the island, and there was so much more for him to do.

He wouldn't leave the island now for anyone.

Except Mila.

He was a zombie by the time the flight landed. His phone was dead, but it was probably best not to announce his arrival to Mila; he'd keep it a surprise in case she tried to escape him. He'd been through that before...never again.

Even his bones were cold by the time he was watching the English scenery float past from a car. And it was raining.

He'd found her mother's address on the system at the MAC, told his team where he was going, left the dogs with Ketut and Wayan...

But he still couldn't quite believe it when he found himself standing on the doorstep of the small redbrick house in Rye.

Amelia Ricci stood up from the bed at the familiar *ding-dong* sound and smoothed down her red-striped skirt. Mila hadn't even noticed before that her mother was all dressed up. She'd been too distracted by her perfume. At first it had smelled so good, but now it was abhorrent to her insides.

'That will be Julian.' Her mother glanced at her in the mirror on the dresser and bouffed up her hair.

Mila fought a smile and placed a hand to her belly. She'd been wondering when this would come up.

'Who's Julian?'

'I wasn't sure things would become serious, so I didn't say anything much to you about him before now, but I think that maybe he's a keeper. He's a doctor, like you—a paediatrician down at St Germaine. Come and meet him.'

Her mother hovered in the doorway.

'On second thoughts, meet him later,' she said.

Mila was grateful. She was happy her mother seemed to have acquired a boyfriend in the time since she'd been gone, but she didn't want to meet him right now.

She had slept for a few hours and showered, and booked an appointment with the family obstetrician, but now it was evening in the UK and her jet lag was playing with her mind as much as the thought of Sebastian, whose phone still appeared to be dead or switched off.

'Will you carry on with this while I'm gone?'

Her mother gestured to the open drawers and

272 ENTICED BY HER ISLAND BILLIONAIRE

boxes, shooting her a look of apprehension. They'd been going through Annabel's stuff. Photos, books, rosettes, love letters still in their envelopes.

'I'm OK with it, Mum,' she said. And she was, she realised.

She heard her mother make a strange sound as she opened the front door downstairs. Mila smiled to herself. Her mother deserved someone who treated her like a goddess. She'd been through so much.

She was studying a photo of herself and Annabel on either side of a man dressed as a giant strawberry when the stairs outside the room creaked again.

'Um… Mila?' Her mother looked quite sheepish, peering around the doorway. 'It wasn't Julian.'

The door opened wide.

Mila stood up in her socks and leggings and her heart started crashing against her ribs even before she saw him.

She dropped the photo.

Sebastian stepped into her old bedroom and the familiar scent of him took her hyperactive nostrils by surprise. It did something strange to her insides, where their baby was—something good—and her eyes clouded over with tears. In a second she was falling against his chest as he stood there in the middle of the floor, on the rug where she'd used to play dolls and cars with Annabel.

'You're here...'

'You gave me no choice.'

'I'm so sorry I left you...' She breathed into his jacket, clutching the lapels and kissing his lips. He was cold; she'd never felt his lips so cold. 'Sebastian, I know it was terrible of me, but I totally freaked out.'

'I know,' he said, putting equally cold hands to her face.

She leaned her cheek against one palm; she had missed him.

'And I know why you're scared of this, Mila, but you can't ever do this to me again. This is something we will deal with together from now on, OK?'

Mila had almost forgotten her mother was there until the doorbell rang again.

'That *will* be Julian. It was nice to meet you, Dr Becker,' she said. 'I'll leave you two to talk.'

Before she left she shot a look of approval at Mila, for Sebastian.

'You were meant to be in Chicago by now,' Mila whispered, stepping back and keeping hold of his hands. She never wanted to let him go.

He looked exhausted and unshaven but utterly perfect—even out of context in the house she'd grown up in. He was wearing jeans and a designer sweater, and a brown leather jacket. Her hands found her belly again. He'd brought a ray of hope with him from the island.

'A strawberry man?' he said now, half smiling as he bent to pick up the photo.

'It was a pick-your-own-strawberries day and he was the mascot,' she explained, running a finger over Annabel's face in the photo.

Her twin was here in this room—she could feel her right now...just as she had sometimes felt her on the island, too. Was this what Annabel wanted? To see her happy with a guy she'd unknowingly approved for Mila years ago?

She would have shivered at the thought before, but maybe she just hadn't wanted to allow herself happiness, she realised. She'd been wrapped up in her guilt over the accident for so long... She had someone else to think about now, though. She was going to need to be strong.

Sebastian scanned the items on the floor, taking in the trophies and trinkets, the weird-looking carved camel Annabel had got from Dubai.

'This was the room we shared till we were eighteen,' said Mila. 'And this is me finally moving on.' She sighed, motioning to the half-empty drawer she'd already sorted through. She smiled tentatively at him. 'Can you ever forgive me?'

'Mila…' he said, shaking his head.

He shut his eyes, dragged a hand across his face, and for a second she thought that maybe he had come here to break things off. That she'd damaged something that couldn't be fixed.

'I was angry with you for keeping the news about our baby from me,' he admitted, chewing his cheek.

Her stomach sank.

'I'm not going to pretend you didn't rip me to shreds. You must know how much I love you. You must also know how much raising a kid with you would be…' He trailed off, as if he couldn't find the words.

She covered her mouth with her hand. She had never heard him tell her he loved her until now. She was utterly shocked at how the words thrilled her.

'It would be the kind of challenge I'm ready for.'

He shook his head again, almost as if he couldn't believe the words coming out of his mouth either. It made her heart soar again.

'I mean, this kid's going to be feral…running about the island with two dogs, all sandy…'

'Let it be feral. I love you, too. Sebastian. I *do* love you. And I know I haven't been the easiest person to deal with, but I'm willing to try and make things work. On the island.'

There was no question in her mind that she'd go back to the island. She missed it already— and the MAC, and little Jack.

'We can do this together if you're really sure it's what you want?'

'*You* are what I want, Mila, and this baby.'

His words were like a confetti bomb going off in her chest and she moved to sit astride him on the edge of the bed, arms and legs wrapped around him.

'I'm so sorry I made you miss your mother's birthday,' she said, kissing him everywhere she could reach, as though he might suddenly disappear in a flash.

She had been through worse, but he was her safe place now. She could feel it—warmth, security and...*home*, she thought. She was home with him.

He let out a sigh into her hair. 'Technically we were supposed to be on that plane to Chicago,' he said, wrapping his hands in her hair, the way he always did. 'But the party's not till Friday, so there's still time for us to get there.'

He kissed her, and the scent of his jacket was driving her hormones crazy.

'You could take me round some of the English countryside, show me off to your friends...'

'Stop talking,' she told him.

She was already sliding his leather jacket off and unbuttoning his shirt.

CHAPTER TWENTY-ONE

SEBASTIAN POPPED THE olive from his virgin martini into his mouth, appreciating Mila from a distance. Her hair was up in a bun again, with soft tendrils framing her face. And she was wearing the fitted blue dress from Bali he'd brought with him—just in case. She looked incredible; she was clearly the best-dressed, most eye-catching woman at the party. But maybe he was biased—she was carrying his baby, after all.

'She seems to have made a good impression on them already,' Jared observed next to him, sipping his own martini. 'Shame you had to move all the way to that island to find her. but still…'

He grinned, slapped his shoulder, and Sebastian shifted on his feet as the box in his jacket pocket dug into his skin.

'I guess this is your way of giving me final brotherly approval,' he said.

'You did the right thing, going to get her,' Jared said seriously.

'I know.'

The party was in full swing. Mila was standing by the buffet table now, chatting happily to Jared's wife Laura and little Charlie, and Sebastian's mother, too. His mother seemed to adore her already.

It hadn't been that tough to convince her to come once he'd shown her a photo of the double bed on the private jet. They'd slept there, eaten caviar, indulged in some other bed-based activities and even watched *Star Wars*—which he'd remembered neither of them had ever seen.

They'd spent part of yesterday quietly breaking the news of her pregnancy to his family. His mother was so excited about being a grandma again she had already asked her assistant to book her a flight to Bali. She had never even been to visit him on the island before, Sebastian realised, but this was not the moment to feel offended.

The crowds seemed to part as he made his way over to Mila.

'Mila Ricci, do I need to tell you how much I love you in that dress?'

She sighed contentedly and leaned against him as he ran a hand gently across her stomach. He still got a kick out of imagining their baby. Boy or girl, he wasn't bothered which—he knew it would be the love of his life…after Mila.

'I'd better wear it some more, before I get too big for it to fit,' she replied, turning in his arms.

'I'll just get you a bigger one made.'

'I'll wear it every day in surgery.'

'You can wear whatever you like under your white coat…or nothing at all.'

She laughed.

He knew his family and the entire badminton club were watching surreptitiously from their various spread-out social circles around the flower-decorated marquee.

Jared had spared no expense, as usual. There were flowers, multiple musical performers—including a six-piece band—a lavish feast to put an eighteenth-century king to shame, and later there would be fireworks in the gardens by the Japanese koi lake to close the monumental evening.

He could tell Mila had been a little surprised by the extravagance, but there was one more thing to do. It was now or never.

His heart sped up as he lowered himself to one knee in front of her.

'Sebastian, what are you…?'

A crowd started gathering and on the orchid-covered stage the band's jovial tune quivered into quiet.

'Sebastian…' Mila had gone red.

Jared handed him a microphone. He'd considered waiting till they were alone, but there were five hundred people gathered here—he had to give them something worth gossiping about.

Slowly he opened the lid of the little black velvet box.

He heard her gasp, watched her eyes pool with tears as she took in the stunning diamond ring set in platinum. He'd had ten diamonds studded around the main one, so it sparkled the way he knew all women dreamed their engagement ring would sparkle. He'd had to wait till Mila had been whisked off by his mother for an anti-jet-lag massage to go and collect it.

'I can't believe this…'

'Mila,' he said, focusing on her face.

She met his eyes and he knew he'd made the right decision. He wanted to cement this *now*.

'I know this has been crazy, and quick, and God knows neither of us expected any of it, but you are the best thing ever to have walked off the boat onto that island and I want you there with me for the rest of our lives.' He took a deep breath. 'Will you do me the immense honour of becoming my wife? Will you marry me?'

Mila looked as if she couldn't speak. For a second he thought maybe he'd gone too far. Someone pulled out a camera, but he saw Jared put a hand across the lens to stop them.

'Mila?'

'Yes, Sebastian—yes! Sorry, I'm in shock. *Yes!* Of course I will marry you.'

They were kissing now, and she was laughing, crying, hugging him. All before he'd even slid the ring on her finger.

'She said yes!' he yelled needlessly to the crowd, pulling her into him again. Relief flooded through him. 'God, I love you when you're blushing,' he growled into her ear.

'Can I get a photo of the happy couple?' someone asked. And suddenly there were cameras everywhere.

Mila stepped in front of him. 'No, thank you, we don't want any photos.'

'It's OK,' he said, taking her hand.

She squinted up at him. 'What do you mean? You hate all this!'

'This is a moment I'm proud of,' he replied decisively, and they happily posed for the crowd, with Mila's ring the centrepiece.

'You've changed,' she teased him.

He rolled his eyes, smiling. He knew people would always gossip, but he'd learned to let it go a little more since Mila had arrived. If she didn't care about the media, why should he care any more? And that little kid's newspaper article had thrown a positive light on his mounting new reputation as an island entrepreneur.

He knew the negative press—if it ever came again—wouldn't affect his work, or the people he loved. That was all that mattered. He had new priorities now.

Jared was at the microphone suddenly, tapping it. Charlie was gripping his father's pocket, holding a toy dinosaur in his other hand.

'Congratulations to my brother and his fiancée Dr Mila Ricci, everybody!'

The crowd went crazy. His mother was wiping tears from her eyes.

'And, seeing as this is a night for announcements, I have one myself,' Jared continued, clearing his throat. 'I am delighted to say happy seventieth birthday to our wonderful, long-suffering mother!'

The applause was rapturous and their mother performed a curtsey, but Jared wasn't done.

'I would also like to say that that this will be the final season of *Faces of Chicago.*'

The gasps around the marquee were audible.

'From early next year I'll be spending more time in Indonesia, concentrating on getting a new Becker Institute facility for wellness and healing up and running. My brother and I...*and* his fiancée...will let you know more as soon as we can. For now, however, I'm sure he'll be busy with wedding plans.'

Sebastian shot Mila a secret smile. Jared had discussed this with them last night, of course, but it still felt strange to know it was actually happening, after all this time.

He'd turned those investors down already, telling them he was keeping this one in the family, and Jared was coming over for three months initially, to partner him on planning, recruitment and development. He and Laura would also look for schools on Bali for Charlie.

'I have a feeling things will be different around the island pretty soon,' Mila said, admiring her ring again.

'I have a feeling you're right,' he said, drawing her closer for a photo with Charlie and his dinosaur.

One year later

Baby Hope Annabel Becker was watching the tiny turtles on the sand with keen interest as Mila sat with her near the surf.

'Do you want to release one?' she whispered, revelling in the baby-soft curls of Hope's hair against her cheek.

They were sitting at the shoreline, barefoot. The moon was high in the sky. The annual sea turtle fundraiser was the perfect opportunity to introduce Hope to the baby turtles who'd grown from eggs in the sanctuary and were now ready to explore their new ocean home around the reef.

'We've released a hundred so far—thanks to Jack, here.' Sebastian grinned as his sandy feet appeared alongside little Jack's in the water. 'He wants to show you this one.'

Little Jack was learning to walk and talk. Wayan looked on from a seat nearby as her son shoved a baby turtle in Mila's face enthusiastically, and she laughed as Wayan rushed over and swept him up, handing the turtle back.

'Was that ice-cream on his face?' Mila asked Sebastian.

Wayan was wiping some kind of smear from Jack's cheek behind them and Sebastian grimaced.

'What can I say? I'm a bad godfather. Good thing I'm so great at everything else.'

Mila laughed and handed him Hope as he sat down beside her. A wave washed up and soaked them fully to their waists. Hope giggled, the way she always did. She loved the ocean.

'Uncy! Uncy!' Jack's vocabulary was improving. He was calling his Uncle Sebastian back already.

'Just taking a moment with my wife, buddy,' he called back. 'And maybe your future girlfriend?'

He glanced down at Hope, put a finger to her tiny hand and winked.

Mila nudged him playfully. 'Are you setting our daughter up already? We're not the only survivors on this island, you know. She'll be free to make her own choice, just like you were.'

'I wasn't free. You trapped me the moment I met you.'

Mila leaned in to kiss him. She didn't care who saw. No one bothered them, and there was no gossip anyway. They were happy together—just a regular couple with a baby—and to everyone else that was probably boring.

They had worked on Jack's cleft lip and palate, reduced his scarring to a minimum, and now he looked like any other rambunctious one-year-old. He was growing as fast as baby Hope.

Everyone on the island seemed to be charting Hope's progress. And luckily for them there was no shortage of willing babysitters, or people to read bedtime stories in the MAC grounds.

When her mother and Julian had visited, they'd started a children's circle—five p.m. on Wednesdays—and Mila had kept it up when they'd left. She still averaged about twenty kids each time.

Sebastian had teased her. 'For someone who said she'd rather have a dog than a family, you now have two dogs and twenty kids!'

'I'm calling this one Sergeant Major,' Sebastian said now, taking Hope's tiny hand and placing it on the turtle's smooth shell.

Mila watched as he dropped a kiss on their baby's head. *If Annabel was here now she'd be so happy to be an auntie*, she mused, just as a yellow butterfly fluttered down and perched on Hope's nose.

Sebastian looked at her. He didn't say it, and neither did she, but butterflies had a habit of landing on Hope. It was mostly whenever Mila thought about her sister...

* * * * *